AUTHOR

The 17 short stories in this b
works from the 1990s to 2015.
lished in print magazines in Indonesia, as well as on my
social media channels.

The inspiration for the stories comes from eavesdropping
on public transportation, articles in newspapers, strangers
I met in coffee shops, and my own family. Thank you for
letting me write them down to be read by many.

I'd like to thank the Emma Press, who believed in this
collection and decided to publish it in English. Thanks
to Ikhda Ayuning Maharsi Degoul and Philippa Barker,
who translated these stories so beautifully.

Thanks to the editors, Georgia Wall and Emma Dai'an
Wright, for being so patient with me.

Thanks to Amy Louise Evans for her beautiful artwork
for the cover.

And thanks to all the beloved readers who decided to read
these stories from Indonesia. Enjoy!

Reda Gaudiamo

JAKARTA, 2023

REDA GAUDIAMO

ABOUT US

TRANSLATED BY

IKHDA AYUNING MAHARSI DEGOUL & PHILIPPA BARKER

THE EMMA PRESS

For my family:
where life begins and love never ends.

THE EMMA PRESS

First published in the UK in 2023 by the Emma Press Ltd.
Originally published in Indonesia as *Tentang Kita* by Stiletto
Book in 2015.

Stories © Reda Gaudiamo 2015.

English-language translation of 'Ayah, Dini and Him',
'Maybe Bib Was Right', 'Her Mother's Daughter', 'Family
Portrait', 'About Us', '24 x 60 x 60', 'The Little One', 'The
Trip', 'Baby', 'Son-In-Law', 'Taxi' and 'Dawn on Sunday' ©
Ikhda Ayuning Maharsi Degoul and Philippa Barker 2023.

English-language translation of 'I Am a Man', 'An Apology',
'Cik Giok', 'Our World' and 'One Fine Morning' © Ikhda
Ayuning Maharsi Degoul 2023.

Edited by Georgia Wall and Emma Dai'an Wright.
Cover design © Amy Louise Evans 2023.

ISBN 978-1-912915-13-2

A CIP catalogue record of this book is available from the
British Library.

Printed and bound in the UK by youloveprint, East Sussex.

The Emma Press
theemmapress.com
hello@theemmapress.com
Birmingham, UK

iv

Contents

Publication of this book was made possible, in part, with assistance from the LitRI Translation Funding Program of the National Book Committee and Ministry of Education and Culture of the Republic of Indonesia.

Ayah, Dini and Him

1. Ayah[*]

The rain is heavy outside, rays of sunlight reflecting off the deep puddles that run like rivers down the street. If anyone dared to cross it, they'd be soaked through at once. A year ago, on a stormy night like this, Dini ran away from home, slamming the door behind her. I should have called out to her, pleaded with her to come inside. I could have gone after her, fetched her back home.

I should have reached for her hand, pulled her close and wrapped her shivering body in a towel. I should have told her, 'Here now, we can put this behind us. We were both angry. Please, forget what I said. Go take a bath before you catch a cold.' And I can picture her smiling up at me, wiping away her tears.

That's what I should have done, but it didn't happen like that. Instead I just sat there, glued to my seat, lips tightly sealed as my fingers gripped the pipe I'd stopped smoking. I didn't move to go after her, didn't say a single thing to bring her back. Dini left and didn't return, and hasn't stepped foot in this house since that day.

I heard about her graphic design business from friends of hers I ran into at the market. I was glad to know it was going well, that a recent collaboration had paid off.

---

[*]   Ayah - father

But when it used to rain like this, back when Dini still came home to visit me, she would put out two glasses of sekoteng and snacks made by Bik Nah, our household help. We would sit together and talk, watching the downpour. Listening to the sound of rain was our secret hobby, our favourite pastime. We loved the atmosphere it created; how it was loud and intense, but also calming. Our conversation always ended up on the same topics: art, design, film, sometimes politics and education too.

We made a good team, Dini and I; we were alike in so many ways. What I'd give now to talk to her again, just the two of us watching the rain. But maybe what I want even more than that is for her to find another man to confide in, a partner for the rest of her life.

'You know, Dini, when you get married someday, our rainy day chats will have to end. Your future husband might not share our hobby,' I told her one cloudy evening.

'Well, guess what? When I get married, I'm going to choose a man just like you, Ayah. And I won't let him interfere with my hobbies. He'll just have to learn to like rainstorms too,' she said heatedly.

'What, you really want to marry a man like me? I'll tell you this: there is no one like me in the whole universe. And even if there was, where would be the fun in that? You'll get bored of me eventually.'

She shook her head. 'I'll never get bored with you, Ayah. And I will find someone who is just like you. And when I do, I won't have to spend time getting used to them, because I know I like you already.'

'Ah, so you just want the easy option?'

'Don't you want me to be happy?' She stared at me with her big round eyes, something in her expression reminding me of her mother. She reached out and hugged me, planting a kiss on my cheek. 'Just you wait and see – my boyfriend will be just like you, Ayah!' Then she released me. 'It's still raining. I want another glass of sekoteng. Do you want more too?' She got up. I could tell she was bored of all our talk of future husbands.

That wasn't the first time we'd talked about when she might settle down and find a husband. We often discussed it, though I was always the one who brought it up. But still the subject was never settled, always skidding to a halt at the same point: she would only consider marrying a man like me. I told myself that things would work themselves out, that she'd find someone eventually. I'll admit I grew impatient though, waiting for that day to arrive.

Dini never brought up the word 'boyfriend' or mentioned any relationships. I knew she had lots of male friends, though she never seemed to pay them much attention. Now she was twenty-five and had finished her studies the previous year, I wondered whether she would finally start to show some interest. She might have seemed indifferent to the idea, but it nagged at me all the time, until one day I began to suspect that there might be someone after all.

I don't recall exactly when, but at some point a particular name began to crop up in Dini's life. While Dini's other male friends rarely came up in conversation, this man was mentioned more and more often.

Every Saturday, and sometimes on a Friday afternoon

when Dini was able to finish work at her studio in Jakarta early, she would come home to Bogor to visit me. But now the evenings we spent together, catching up on each other's lives as we walked the quiet streets of Sempur, were shared by the three of us. Me, Dini, and him.

We could still talk about the same things, because he claimed to have the same interests as Dini and me. But when our talk drifted onto the topic of graphic design, he began to dominate the conversation, like he couldn't contain his opinions a moment longer. Knowing the field quite well, I didn't buy everything he said, whereas Dini, who'd studied visual and graphic design for years at the Institute of Technology in Bandung, couldn't stop asking him questions, hanging off his every word.

What had happened to my bright girl who could think for herself? Had she forgotten everything she'd learned? Dini lapped up every supposed fact and figure that fell from his mouth. I grew tired of his foolishness, tired of watching Dini say 'Oh!' and 'Wow!' and 'Really?' over and over, like she was stuck on repeat. Once, when my ears were unable to listen to him rattle on a moment longer, I excused myself early, hoping that Dini would take the hint and ask him to call it a night. But without me there, their conversation became even more lively, his voice growing in volume as he told story after story.

Back in my room, I could still hear Dini's laughter. Rage thumped in my chest as I thought about how he'd deliberately and skilfully ejected me from the conversation with his tedious talk about graphic design, and then moved on to other topics once I'd gone. I was going to have to keep an eye on him, that was for sure.

Lying awake in the middle of the night, I listened to the sound of Dini's laughter as it carried through the house. Though the room was dark, I saw my bedroom door slowly open as Dini peered inside. I quickly shut my eyes and pretended to be asleep, until I heard the door swing shut again.

'You'd better stay with me, Yos,' she whispered, failing to suppress a giggle. 'Ayah is fast asleep and snoring already.'

Snoring? Me? How dare you, Dini!

2. Dini

It's hot as a sauna outside, though it's been raining for four solid days now. Luckily Bang Ucup helped me check the roof of my studio last week, or there might have been trouble.

The din of water falling on the rooftops tells me the rain is still heavy. But with the street empty of people, it's also eerily quiet. As I sit and listen to the rain, coffee growing cold, my thoughts drift to Ayah. I picture him sitting in the living room of our family home, sipping on a glass of sekoteng, a plate of fried sweet bananas on the table beside him. I wonder if he still enjoys a good rainstorm like we used to.

This wasn't always our favourite pastime. It began twelve days after Ibu, my mother, was buried. When the rain that had started early in the morning showed no sign of stopping, Ayah decided to stay home for the day. I remember he sat in the living room flipping through an old magazine of Ibu's, his gaze occasionally drifting to stare out the window. With no interesting books to read, I resorted to playing 'Autumn Leaves' – Ibu's favourite song, which I knew by heart – on the piano till I got bored.

I sat down next to Ayah. Unable to find any words, neither of us said anything for a while, until we both took a breath at the same time. Ayah smiled at me before he began to talk.

'It's so calm, isn't it, Dini?'

'Yes, Ayah. I can't stop thinking about Ibu. Are you thinking about her too?'

He nodded. 'Come, tell me a story, Din.'

His request surprised me. 'What kind of story, Ayah?'

'Anything you like. You used to love chatting with your mother. What kind of things did you share with her?'

It felt strange, talking to Ayah like that. It was as though I was in front of a stranger – I didn't know what to say. But he was patient, encouraging me to try talking to him instead now that Ibu was gone.

And so I began to share every bit of my life with him: stories about my school friends, the stern teachers, my ever-growing pile of homework, and my worries about the upcoming exams. When it was his turn, he told me about his work, letting me into the art world I had always been so curious about.

Ibu had always told me that Ayah's job was boring, though Ayah did his best to defend it, trying to convince me of its appeal. He would often keep himself busy in the room Ibu nicknamed his 'warehouse', though Ayah had made a sign saying 'studio' and fixed it to the door. Sometimes his friends would come and visit his studio, to take a look at his work. I could tell that this made him happy because of the smile on his face after their visits.

On the last day of rain after Ibu's passing, I came to appreciate Ayah's job in all its wonder. I finally saw how, with paint, a brush and canvas, you could create the most beautiful artworks. When I graduated from high school a year later, I broke the promise I had made to Ibu to go on to study economics and chose fine art instead.

To my surprise, Ayah disagreed, insisting that I keep the promise I'd made to Ibu all those years ago. He was angry when he found out that I'd only applied to study fine art at the Institute of Technology in Bandung, and nowhere else.

'If there are still private universities open for a second wave of applications, I'd like you to apply, just in case.' He looked serious. 'Only applying to ITB... I'm sorry, but I'm not happy about that.'

I couldn't figure him out. It was Ayah who had unlocked my passion for art. Now I'd fallen in love with it and didn't want to let go of my dream, he was forcing me to leave it behind.

'But why, Ayah?' The deadline for the second wave of applications had passed already. Plus, deep down, I knew I didn't want to go to any other university. I cried every day for a week as I argued with him, until finally something in his heart melted. From then on, we resumed our conversations about art as if nothing had happened. I left for university soon after, and then after graduating I got a job in a small studio in Jakarta.

I was quite sure that I would never find a man as great as Ayah, until Yos came into my life. He arrived at a time when I desperately needed someone to help me design adverts in the studio. Sure, I had friends who came and helped out, but they were students, like I had once been. Reliable only until exams started, when they would leave the studio to study.

I finally decided to put an advert on the information board at Graha Bhakti Budaya opera house. It was small, almost invisible among the many others. By the seventh day, when there were still no applications, I had almost given up. But then on the eighth Yos arrived.

'I'll be honest with you, I don't have any formal education in graphic design,' he said in the interview.

'I don't mind that. What I'm interested in is your style, creativity and work ethic. Also, your relationships with clients. I'm a small business owner and I care about my clients. We work very closely with them on projects.'

'I can't guarantee that my style will be to your taste, but if you give me some work I'll show you what I can do. Here, look at my portfolio. And in terms of collaboration, I'm always professional in my relationships. Nothing more, nothing less.'

'And you're disciplined?'

'I meet all my deadlines, if that's what you mean.'

He smiled at me.

At that moment, I knew I'd chosen the right person.

He was the man I wanted to work with. Yos always came up with brilliant ideas, things I'd never thought of before. With simple tools and equipment, he was able to tackle complicated tasks. Not to mention his passion for photography.

'Yos, what made you want to work here?' I asked one day. 'With your skills, you could have found a good position at a big advertising agency where you'd get paid millions of rupiahs.'

'It wasn't for me, Dini,' he said. 'They're looking for highly-qualified fine art graduates, but they also want you to specialise. Their art directors don't get to do photography as well as drawing and writing. But I like doing all those things. And anyway, they don't hire people over 30 for starter roles. Honestly, I almost gave up trying to find a new job after leaving my publishing position, and then I saw the advert you'd put in Taman Ismail Marzuki.'

'Well that would have been daft! What if I hadn't hired you? What would you have done then?'

'Probably the same as I've always done – just taken the first job I found. The pay can be good. But it's so tiring – jobs come and go so fast. Nothing's certain,' he said, laughing. He told me stories about his time at other jobs and things that had gone wrong, though he made them sound funny rather than traumatic.

The studio always kept us busy. Sometimes we stayed late to finish projects, working through to the early hours of the morning. Those nights brought us closer together, and then one day Yos told me about his feelings for me.

Fortunately, or perhaps unfortunately, since we were co-workers, I felt the same for him. I was nervous, wondering how I'd tell Ayah. I wanted Ayah to know that I'd met a smart, skilful, knowledgeable, kind man, just like him. How happy he would be, I thought. I wanted to tell him right away.

But I was wrong. Not only was Ayah displeased when I told him about Yos, but he was actively against him. And just like when I'd chosen to study at ITB, Ayah insisted that I let Yos go.

'Find another man. Whoever you want, but not this man.'

'Why? What's wrong with Yos? You don't even know him. You don't see his talent. I see you in him. Of course, you're not exactly the same, but he –'

'Please stop comparing us, Dini. You need to find the best way to end your relationship with him. There are many talented people in this world who would make good co-workers. I can help you find a replacement, if you want.'

'I'm not doing anything until you tell me why you hate Yos.' My voice was trembling and I could feel tears welling in my eyes, but I refused to back down – not until I understood why Ayah felt the way he did. But he wouldn't explain his reasoning, and just carried on insisting.

'Ayah, you're not going to back down, but nor will I. Don't be surprised if I marry Yos one day!'

'You wouldn't dare, Dini.' His voice grew sharp, his eyes turning cold with hurt.

'Why not? You'll see!'

'You're so stubborn! But you'll regret it, I guarantee it!'

'I won't! You'll be the one who's sorry!'

It rained heavily that night. I'd told Ayah my news, thinking it would make him smile. I'd imagined him hugging me tight and kissing my cheek, full of joy. But it hadn't gone like that at all. Unable to stop my tears from falling, I grabbed my bag and ran from the house, out into the downpour. All the while Ayah sat in his chair, glued to the spot.

3. Dini and Him

'Yos, you startled me!'

'I knew you wouldn't have gone to bed yet. I always know where you are when it's raining like this. Sat by the window, lost in your thoughts.'

'Will you sit with me for a bit? There's ginger tea in my blue Thermos if you want some?'

'Of course. It's ok, I can get it.'

'Yos, I can't stop thinking about Ayah.'

'He's probably thinking about you too right now. Think about how long it's been since you left. You don't even send him updates, poor guy.'

'If he wants to talk, he can come to me. He's the reason I left.'

'But you're his only child. You know what his temper's like. Why don't you reach out to him?'

'No way. Not until he writes me a letter, or calls and explains everything.'

'Everything?'

'Yes, everything about you, about us!'

'Ah, so it's that. He must have a good reason for not

liking me. Parents always have strong views, especially about their future sons-in-law.'

'Don't you mind that he hates you?'

'Of course I do. I'm not thrilled about it. You did warn me about what he was like, though. But the way he's gone about things, trying to split us up... Of course it hurts. Why do you think he hates me so much, Din?'

'I've got no idea. I just can't think why.'

'Maybe he hates smokers?'

'Nonsense. He used to smoke a lot himself. He still loves smoking his pipe. He always said he'd stop, but he still hasn't. No, he definitely doesn't hate smokers.'

'Maybe it's because I'm from a different ethnicity and background to him?'

'But that's ridiculous. Ayah and Ibu weren't of the same ethnicity. It never bothered him before.'

'Maybe it didn't back then, but he could have changed his mind. Maybe he secretly hoped his son-in-law would come from the same place as him, so he'd know his family and background already?'

'I'm telling you, it doesn't matter to him!'

'Hey, for all we know that could be the reason, Dini.'

'Maybe. But if it was, it would scare me how narrow-minded and petty he'd become.'

'Look, I can't pretend to know what's going on in his head. But I'm sure it hurt him a lot.'

'Yes, I don't want us to...'

'Let's not overthink it. Everything will be fine.'

'But how?'

'We'll go and see him.'

'You really want to?'

'Yes. I mean, why not? Maybe he'll explain himself.'

'No, I don't think I can face it.'

'What are you afraid of? I haven't done anything wrong. I just want to know the truth. If he has a good reason and I agree with him, then maybe we'll have to reconsider our relationship.'

'Hang on, what? You would really do that?'

'Let's be realistic, though. It's probably just a misunderstanding.'

'So –'

'So, I'd like to go and see your father, if I may? I can go on my own, or would you rather come with me?'

'Errr...'

'Though maybe it's better if you don't come.'

'Yes, I'd prefer to wait here.'

'Okay then. That's what we'll do.'

4. Ayah and Him

'What are you doing here? Is Dini not with you? Don't tell me she's too scared to see me?'

'She's tied up at the studio, Pak.'*

'Well then, how can I help you?'

'I've come because I want answers. I know you don't approve of our relationship. You've made it very clear you don't like me and Dini being together. But I want to know why.'

---

*   Pak - sir

'It's not something I'm willing to discuss any further.'

'Why not?'

'Because I don't want to.'

'But how can I begin to understand things from your point of view if you won't at least explain? You must see that your decision doesn't just affect you. It affects Dini and me, and we have a right to know.'

'Don't try and manipulate me.'

'You've put me in this position, Pak.'

'It's not easy to explain. I wouldn't know where to start.'

'I'll listen. I'll try to understand.'

'Are you serious about Dini?'

'Yes, Pak, I'm serious.'

'Do you love her? Will you support her, wherever life takes her?'

'Yes, with all my heart and soul.'

'Are you sure?'

'Yes.'

'You and your big head. You're just an employee in her business. Did you know she founded the studio all by herself? She used her own money, plus a little from her mother. And then you came along, got a job there, told her you love her, and now I hear you plan to marry her. You think everything's going to be rosy, don't you? Are you really that stupid?'

'What? I don't understand –'

'You've got no idea how strong and tough my little girl is. She's ambitious, just like her mother. Whatever she sets her mind to, it's hers. She's always been successful, up to now. Always.'

'She's an incredible woman.'

'I couldn't agree more. But then I see who you are. Dini's told me all about you. You're all she's talked about these past few months, before she left. I've heard all about your failures. I've heard all about the countless jobs you've had, and yet here you are with nothing to show for it. And now you, you with your fancy adverts, you dare to take my talented daughter away from me. I can't believe your nerve!'

'Pak…'

'Don't interrupt me. I know what's going to happen next. This is all going to end in tears. I'm sorry, but you're on a sinking ship. I know because I was in the same position myself once. I don't want that life for my daughter.'

'Maybe it was you who got it wrong, Pak.'

'How dare you!'

'I'm sorry, Pak, but how can you know what tomorrow will bring? You seem so confident in predicting where our relationship is headed, but it's our life, mine and Dini's, not yours. Yes, I work for Dini, but it doesn't mean I'm beneath her. We do different tasks according to our skills, but we see each other as equals. We're not just co-workers, we're partners. If you think I begged her to take me on, or that I'm holding her back, you're wrong. And as for what 'we' are, we're not just co-workers. We are lovers who work together. And we're determined to take the business forward and keep getting better.'

'Big words, Yos!'

'Pak –'

'Listen to me. They used to be my words too. I used to say the exact same things. That's right. We'd say them too, me and Mira, Dini's mother. Decades ago, before we were even married, we had exactly the same dream as yours. Mira loved my paintings – she wanted to open a gallery to show off my work. But it never happened. My paintings couldn't provide enough for us to live on. Mira had to find a different job to help keep us afloat. And she was good at it, getting promotion after promotion while my paintings faded into obscurity. People saw me as the man who lived off his wife's earnings. They judged me for that, and they were right. Mira was the one bringing in the money. She was the one responsible for providing for our family all those years. She paid for Dini's education. I never contributed a penny. But Mira, she never complained. She always told me how proud she was of me, of my paintings. But how could I believe her? Deep down, I knew how disappointed she was with me. How frustrated she was with the way life had turned out.'

'Did you ever talk to her about it?'

'What would have been the point? To upset her further? No. I already knew how she felt. The proof came when she suggested we keep Dini away from the art world, in case she decided she wanted to be an artist too. We could see she had a natural talent for it, but I didn't want her to have the same experience as I had. We wanted Dini to live a good life, to thrive and be successful, to find a man who would make her happy. I can't bear to see our life story repeat itself in hers.'

'But, Pak –'

'Let me finish. And then you show up, and I see myself in you like it was yesterday. Don't you see? You're working for a woman, you say as equals, but it's her business. Can you handle that? Could you cope with what people might say? I'm worried for my daughter. I don't want Dini to feel guilty for being more talented or successful than her husband. I don't want her to hold herself back from dreaming big because she's scared she'll leave you behind. I just want her to…'

'You want her to be happy, and successful, I understand that. But Pak, do you think this can only happen if we split up?'

'Yes. I don't want to see you fail like me. That will hurt her so much. And I don't want Dini to hold back her career because of you. That would hurt her twice over. So once more, I ask you, please leave my daughter alone. Please, let her go. Let her go her own way, and you yours.'

'Wait, Pak…'

'I think we're done here. Go home, young man. Good night.'

5. Ayah, Dini and Him

It's a rainy day in Bogor.

The old man sits in his living room, enjoying the view out of the window through the raindrops. His mug of wedang jahe* grows cold on the table, but he doesn't seem to care.

It's been three days since he had his last visitor, the young man who came and heard what was in his heart. He regrets it now, sharing his story of failure. The young

---
*   Wedang jahe - hot ginger tea

man will have told Dini, and now his little girl will never look at him in the same way again. She will only see him as an old man who was always a loser, who was always in the shadow of his wife. What would Mira say to him, he who promised to steer their daughter safely onto a different path? The past has come back to haunt him, leaving them at an impasse.

If only the young man were rich, and not an artist, then he'd happily let his only daughter go. But he won't let his daughter feel guilty for striding ahead of her husband, for being the one who succeeds. He doesn't want Dini to feel the pain that Mira felt, letting opportunities and promotions go because she was afraid they would distance her from her husband. He feels sorry for the young man, he honestly does. But he can't set him up to fail, to live his life in second place. They should break up now, and go their own way. He wants that so badly.

His thoughts are interrupted as a bemo* slows to a stop at the fence. Who would come by on a rainy day like this? He spots two figures in raincoats hurrying out, opening the gate and running up towards the house.

'Ayah!'

He knows that voice. It's Dini's. She is with the young man, on the other side of the glass door. He stands up quickly, unlocking the door, and then wet hands are grabbing his hands, hugging him. A wet face is kissing his cheek, and another pair of arms are around his shoulders.

'Yos told me everything, Ayah!'

---

*   Bemo - a three-wheeled taxi

'I knew it. So what next? Have you come here to gang up on me?' He studies the face of the young man to see if he's angry, but he only finds a smile.

'Come, let's sit down, Ayah. Yos, please close the door.'

'I gather you have something important to tell me.'

'Yes, Ayah.'

'You've decided to split up? Is that right?' He sees his daughter's eyes sparkle as she watches the young man return from closing the door.

'I'm sorry to break it to you, Pak, but the answer is no.' The young man is calm. 'We're staying together, for good.'

'But why? It's a terrible idea. Why come back again if you still won't listen? Was I not clear enough the first time round?'

'Because we know we're made for each other.'

'Don't be so naïve. You think your mother and I didn't believe exactly the same thing? And just look at what happened. I don't think you understood a word I said to you, young man.'

'I understood, Pak, but I believe the opposite is true.'

'Ayah, your story gave us faith that we can make this work. We've discussed any doubts we had and we're committed to finding a path that's right for us.'

'Dini, you don't know what you're talking about.'

'Pak, we're not interested in competing with one another. And we're not going to hold each other back either. We're committed to helping each other be the best we can be, and that only makes us stronger. Please, let us prove to you that you have nothing to worry about. I promise I won't let you know. I won't let Dini down.'

'Please, Ayah, we don't want to fight. We've come to ask for your blessing. We don't want to be estranged from you any longer.'

These young people have some nerve, thinks the old man. He stares at the young man in front of him, at his rain-soaked hair, at the spark in his eyes. He takes a deep breath. Then he listens to his heart. Maybe, after all, it's him who's the coward. Who is he to burden this young couple with his fears? That would be wrong. Why not give them the chance to find their own way instead?

The old man stands, pulling a third rattan chair up to the table. He can see his daughter's lips quivering. He taps the young man on the shoulder and pulls his daughter into a tight hug. The rain is pouring down outside.

'Bik, please bring us some wedang jahe, two glasses. Hurry!' he calls, raising his voice to Bik Nah. 'And two big towels, warm ones.'

'Yes, Pak!' she replies, and cups clink faintly in the kitchen.

Maybe Bib Was Right

The morning begins as it always does. Ibu* starts her busy day by opening the gates out front, fetching the newspaper from the letterbox, and then getting on with washing and drying the dishes. Except today Ibu looks clumsier. She walks so slowly.

As usual, Bib has something to say about it: 'Ibu is definitely still tired and sleepy.'

'What did you say? Ibu is still sleepy? That's not like her at all. I know she never stops. If Ibu is tired and sleepy, she should go back to bed, her nice warm bed, instead of busying herself with breakfast like she's doing now.'

Bib shrugs and stops grumbling.

'Ibu does look tired though. And she's wheezing!'

'Where is she?' Bib jumps off the couch and comes over, peering out from behind the curtains. 'Maybe she's been doing some exercises?' he guesses. He takes a deep breath.

'What are you on about? One minute you're saying she's tired and the next you're saying she's off doing exercises? Make your mind up. You want to know what I think? Ibu is too old now to be doing all that housework. She's up at the crack of dawn, before the sun is even up, making sure the gates are open for Mak Pipit, who helps with the laundry, ironing and cleaning. Then she's off to the market, then back home to cook, translate scripts, type them up and take them to the post office, and then she gets din-

---

*   Ibu - mother, or Mrs (Bu for short)

ner ready for the whole family. And she has to make sure all the electricity and phone bills are paid each month.'

'And she's always having to mop up the dirty floors every time we sneak into the living room after playing outside,' says Bib, quietly. He is looking at me. I just grimace. It always surprises me how much mess we leave outside the kitchen, every time we come into the house.

'I thought that Ina, Ita or Aldo could help Ibu with her chores. They're grown up now, aren't they?' Bib says.

'Yes, but they're always busy with their own things.'

'But helping Ibu a little in the mornings wouldn't take too much of their time! Or they could help her to pay the phone and electricity bills. Or couldn't they at least take her translation work to the post office? I mean, they have to pass the post office anyway on the way to their college or work, don't they? Don't they care about Ibu at all? She goes to bed late every night, always waiting up to check they're back home safe. What are they even up to, staying out so late? It's not like they're in college from eight in the morning till eleven at night. But sometimes they're not home until two or three in the morning! That can't be right, can it?'

Listening to Bib go on and on usually drives me crazy, but today I don't stop him.

'Once Bapak was gone, the kids tried to keep themselves busy. They ended up leaving Ibu to do everything herself. Maybe it was good for her, at least for a bit, to distract her from missing Bapak.'

'I don't think that's right. I think it's only made her busier and her life more difficult to manage. Aldo has forgotten that he should help Ibu with her chores.'

'And what about Ina and Ita?'

'Ina is always busy at the office. If she has any free time, she spends it playing on her computer. And Ita? She's always busy with her boyfriend, who's always making her cry.'

'And what about Aldo? What's he up to when he's not at college?'

'I expect he does whatever teenage boys do. Wandering around, hanging out in the mall, bothering pretty girls. Just like I've seen you doing when our neighbour comes past our house.'

'Shut it!' says Bib, though I notice he's smiling. Usually he says my joking around is a bad habit, though I think it's normal for my age.

'Poor Ibu. I wish we could help her.'

'There must be something we can do for her,' Bib whispers. 'I just can't think what…'

Aha! This is the first time Bib hasn't known what to do! Usually he always has a brilliant idea or some madcap theory. But do they work? Ha! Let me think…

I remember the time Bib came up with a plan to drive away the fat rat and his family that lived behind the woodpile under Aldo's window. We just had to mimic the 'extra-special sound' that can only be heard by mammals, he said. I agreed to go along with him. Armed with his brilliant plan, we went and tried with all our might to make the special sound. It went well! But did it drive away the rats? No! All we succeeded in doing was waking up the entire household, and the neighbours too.

That 'extra-special mammal sound' hadn't worked at

all. Ibu, Bapak, Ina, Ita and Aldo stared down at us with sour faces for days. Suddenly we were getting half-portions on our plates. And the rat family was still there, living in peace. That was a great idea, Bib! Thank you!

The gate opens and Mak Pipit appears in the yard. Mak Pipit is basically a good person. But she never smiles at either of us. Every time she is sweeping the floor, she glares at us with angry eyes and a furrowed brow. Bib says it's because she is not happy about the incredibly dirty floor. He says it's my fault, that I'm a scrubby, messy little kid. That's pretty rude! How dare you, Bib!

I try and catch a glimpse of Ibu again from behind the curtain. She looks a bit calmer now. But her face is still pale. Mak Pipit is struggling with the gates, unable to open them any wider. Ibu must have forgotten to unhook the latch. I call out to Ibu. Oh no, I was trying to keep my voice low but I startled her! She nearly fell off her chair. Bib steps on my foot. He saw it too.

'Next time, be quieter. Just whisper!' he growls.

'Whisper? But how?'

Ibu walks slowly over to open the front door. Mak Pipit smiles hello with her shiny yellow teeth. Ibu nods then goes back to sit in the living room. She looks exhausted. Mak Pipit, looking hurt not to get a smile back, goes straight to the kitchen, forgetting to close the door behind her. This is a rare opportunity. I am walking through, ready to go straight to the kitchen. But for some reason I stop. I come closer to Ibu.

The woman looks so old and tired. She's got so many wrinkles and deep lines on her face. So many that I lose count. Her skin looks grey and her lips are trembling. Bib is behind me now. 'I think we should stay with her,' he whispers. 'I'm worried she might faint.'

I agree. I feel her tiny wrinkled hand patting my shoulders and back. She is trying to smile. Bib gently lowers himself onto her feet. She smiles again. Her forehead is sweating. Gradually her patting weakens. Her hands are cold and clammy.

I raise my head. I see she's smiling widely. I wonder if she's trying to say something to me. I poke Bib's back. We are both waiting for some words to come out of her mouth. But she just keeps smiling. Her hand is slowly stroking my back... and then it stops. It rests on my shoulder. It's so heavy I can't move my head. Bib suddenly wakes up from on top of her feet. Oh my goodness, Bib!

'Jig, get up. Something's wrong,' he whispers.

'Don't do anything stupid, Bib! If Mak Pipit comes in now you'll be on half rations for the rest of your life!'

'Jig, this is serious. Can't you feel her hands? They're cold as ice. I'm afraid she might be –'

'What are you talking about, Bib? Wait a minute!' I try to get out from under Ibu's hand. I see that she's sound asleep. Her face looks so chalky and wan. Her lips are still smiling. But it looks different to her smile before. I worry that Bib's theory might be correct.

'Put your nose up to her cheek and breathe a little. If her eyes move at all we'll know she just fell asleep.'

'And what if they don't, Bib?'

'We'll have to wake up the rest of the house.'

I do what Bib tells me. I try to blow on her cheek again

and again. Bib pokes me in the back. I get it. It's time to wake all the people up. Ibu's heart has decided to stop beating.

They groan as we wake them, shouting at us to quieten down. Aldo calls Mak Pipit to come and take us away. I push Bib towards the living room. But Ina and Ita are smart.

'Maybe something's happened,' Ina says, following behind Bib. 'Let's see what they're trying to show us.'

They scream just as I did when they see Ibu in the chair. They are crying so much. Mak Pipit runs to and fro. There is panic and confusion. Once she's calmed down, Ina starts to call everyone who needs to know. Then she makes the necessary arrangements.

All the guests begin to arrive at the house. From what they're saying, it seems Ibu had a heart attack. They also talk about us. Bib says they're talking about how it was the two of us who found her in her last moments of suffering.

Aldo, Ita and Ina stand together, bodies trembling. I see them pulling each other close for hugs, blaming themselves for what happened. Aldo can't forgive himself for refusing to help his mother type up her scripts. Ina wishes she had talked to Ibu more often. And now Ita is whispering to herself in the corner of the living room, wondering if she could have organised her time better, so she could have helped her mother with the housework. 'If only, if only,' they whisper over and over again.

People come and go all week, sending their deepest condolences. Tears roll and roll. Me and Bib don't know what to do so we just lie under their chairs. It goes on and on.

A week later. Mak Pipit arrives early in the morning as usual. Aldo opens the gate for her now. Our food is all prepared. Ina has done all of Ibu's housework perfectly. Everything feels back to normal. All of it. But still, something has changed. There will be no more beautiful voice coming from the kitchen in the morning. No one greeting us with a lovely loud voice: 'Hello there, my naughty little boys!' Our home feels so empty and deserted now.

Maybe it's our fault. Ibu had needed help for a long time. We knew this, but we were never brave enough to tell her children. We should have done something before it was too late. At least we could have reminded them that Ibu was old and tired. But how could we? Every time we tried to tell them, they told us to be quiet. Bib told me his theory again. He says it's because we're only Bib and Jig, the family dogs. Maybe Bib was right.

Her Mother's Daughter

1978

'What did you get in the test?'

'Five point five.'

'Five?'

'Five point five is nearly six, Ibu.'

'Says who? If it was five point eight or nine, then perhaps it could be rounded up to six. But five point five is still only five!'

'…'

'You only scored four on your last test. And now you've just scraped a five point five. I dread to think how your Maths report is going to read at the end of the year. I'm very concerned indeed.'

'…'

'I'm disappointed in you. I know you can do better than this. You're capable of scoring higher. You could have got eight or nine if you'd put in the effort. The problem is you're too lazy to learn. If I don't keep on hassling you, keep getting on your back, you won't study hard enough.'

'…'

'When I was your age, my marks in Maths were never less than eight. Now, I'm not asking you to get eight. I could settle for seven. I'm saying this for your own good. It's not beyond you to get a seven, is it?'

'…'

1983

'I want to do Languages, Bu.'

'Languages? What languages?'

'I mean, I want to choose Language class.'

'Oh, that. Why don't you choose Science class instead? It looks better, don't you think?'

'But Ibu, my teacher said he thought I'd do well in Languages.'

'How can he say that? How well does he really know you?'

'He looked at the results of my IQ test, Bu.'

'Ah, but this IQ test is just made up by the school. You think it will be 100% correct? What about me, your mother? Don't you think I know what's good for you, better than any test? And I say the science option is the perfect fit. You've always shown an interest in chemistry and experiments. And you'll get to learn all about anatomy by dissecting frogs and birds. You could go on to be a doctor, an engineer, a veterinarian… Anything you want.'

'But, Ibu…'

'I will come into school and talk to your principal. I'll explain you're more than capable of taking Science.'

'But –'

'I'm not saying there's anything wrong with the language option, but it won't get you anywhere. You have potential. It would be a shame to waste your intelligence on such trivial lessons. If you start putting in the effort, you'll have no problem achieving great things in life. Now, I'll come in to school tomorrow and see that you're enrolled in Science.'

'But Ibu…'

'No more arguing. You'll do well in this class. You just lack the proper motivation. You spend too much time playing. And too much time talking on the phone.'

'…'

'I'm not asking a lot of you. I've just always dreamt of having a doctor in the family someday, that's all. Why don't you want to take Science?'

'…'

1994

'Bu, the clinic I'm setting up with my friends will be opening soon.'

'Praise the Lord!'

'Maybe you could be our advisor?'

'Of course! When is the opening? And where is the clinic going to be?'

'It's not quite finished yet, Bu. You'll have to be patient. We're hoping it'll be ready by the end of the year.'

'I have an idea. Why not use the pavilion in our yard to set up a clinic for yourself and your friends?'

'We decided not to use our homes for our business, Ibu.'

'Well then, where will it be? Have you rented an office space in a grand building somewhere? That would be splendid. Yes, that would be very prestigious.'

'Not exactly… It's not actually in a building.'

'Well where is it then? Aren't you going to tell me?'

'It's in the fishing village, where I was working as an intern.'

'My goodness! Lord have mercy!'

'What's wrong, Ibu?'

'So it's not a specialist clinic?'

'Yes, it is.'

'But it's in…'

'Yes, Ibu, in a fishing village. What's wrong with that?'

'May the Lord have mercy upon us!'

'Aren't you happy about it?'

'Why spend all those years at school, if you're only going to end up in a fishing village? When will you ever be successful?'

'When will I be rich, don't you mean?'

'Yes, rich. When will you be rich? Living comfortably, without having to worry about money? Don't you want to be like your uncle? He's a dermatologist with wealthy clients who throw their money at him to make them look more beautiful.'

'That's not the kind of work I want to do, Bu.'

'I don't know what's gotten into you. When did you become such a socialist? This is exactly what your father was like. And see where that got him. His life was so unlucky. So hopeless, always asking for help.'

'Come on, Ibu! Years ago, you told me you'd always dreamt of having a doctor in the family. Well, here you are. I'm a doctor now. And I've decided to use my knowledge to actually help people. But yet again, you won't let me make my own decisions.'

'You think you're so clever, don't you? If I'd have known how devious you were, I would never have let you out of my sight. You'd have been better off illiterate. I should never have sent you to school, should never have encouraged you to become a doctor. What an utter waste of time. All that money down the drain. It was all for nothing!'

'...'

'I can see you're grown up now. You want to live your own life and make your own decisions. But you have to believe me – yes, me, your own mother. I'm the only one who knows what you need. And what you definitely don't need is to go building a clinic in a crummy fishing village!'

'...'

'I just want you to be happy.'

'...'

'And don't you want me to be happy too? You know I never ask much of you. So please, don't resign yourself to working in that kampung.* It would be such a shame, after so many years of studying. So much time and energy. All that money on a first-class education, just to end up treating people who can't even pay for your services? What a waste! Come on, why not open a normal clinic like the other doctors we know? A nice orderly clinic that will provide you with a good income. Doesn't that sound like a good idea? It will make you much happier in the long run – not to mention rich.'

1999

'Do you remember Bu Sis? Her daughter is getting married next week.'

---

*   Kampung - village

'Which daughter?'

'The little youngest one.'

'Sri?'

'Yes, her.'

'Oh dear, but she's so young!'

'You say it like it's a bad thing. How old are you now? You're going to turn 30 this year. Look at Bu Sis's first daughter, Yani: she's a year younger than you, and she has three kids already. Three! And what about you? You don't even have a boyfriend!'

'Not now, Bu.'

'Then when are we going to talk about it? Every time I bring it up, you brush me off. How long am I supposed to wait? Do you want me to wait until I die? Until I'm buried in the ground, reunited with Mother Earth?'

'Ibu!'

'I'm sick and tired of waiting. All you think about is your job and your spotty-faced patients. Why not take some time off to find yourself a boyfriend? What's the worst that could happen? Worst case, they get a few more pimples in your absence. It's not like they're going to keel over and die when you're not around.'

'My patients aren't the issue, Bu.'

'No? Because the way I see it, your clinic and patients are exactly what the issue is. You're always so busy working. You never make time to go out and meet anyone, to find yourself a good man.'

'Sure, Bu, but...'

'Sure? What are you so sure about? It won't happen unless you make it a priority. Listen, you can come to the next arisan* with me and meet with the rest of the family. Your aunts and uncles can help. I'm certain they'll know of plenty of potential suitors for you.'

'Bu...'

'You can tell me... If you'd rather not choose yourself, or if you don't feel able, I can find a husband for you. I can sort it all out.'

'But what if we're not right for one another?'

'Impossible! I'll find the perfect match for you. Do you think I'd choose the wrong suitor for my own child?'

'But what if we're not a good match? You can't force that.'

'Good match, bad match, it's all down to you. Trust me. Believe in the match and your marriage will be a success.'

'I don't know, Bu. It feels really weird.'

'Will you stop being so stubborn? For once in your life, what about doing something that brings me a little joy? I never ask anything of you. But I want you to find a husband. I want you to get married. I just want you to be happy? What's wrong with that?'

2002

'Tante Nik just had another grandchild today. So she has four grandchildren now.'

'Wow, they must have their hands full.'

'Not at all. It's brought them much joy. They have so much fun together!'

'...'

---

*   Arisan - a gathering that involves a lottery of some sort

'I also dreamt of having grandchildren.'

'…'

'Look, how old are you now? What are you waiting for? Better to have children now, before it's too late. You'll regret it if you don't.'

'Can't we wait a little while, Bu? Everything's going so well at the moment.'

'Oh, but there will never be a perfect time. You'll never feel ready. You should have a baby now, while you're both still young. It will only get more difficult as you get older.'

'Not yet, Bu.'

'What are you waiting for? Do you want to see me die before you give me grandchildren? How can you be so cruel? I've never asked you to build me a big house, or to pay for me to travel and see the world. I've never asked you for expensive jewels, not once! I just want you to give me grandchildren! Even just one grandchild, while God still gives me a chance to live! Is that too much to ask?'

'…'

2006

'So, when can I expect my second grandchild?'

'…'

'Next year, perhaps?'

'…'

'They would be so cute, so adorable together. It's the best idea!'

'Maybe there won't be another, Ibu.'

'What? That's impossible. You're just going have the one child?'

'Yes. It's looking that way.'

'But I'll be so lonely with just one. You'll be lonely too!'

'It's ok, Bu. We'll be fine.'

'How can you say that? It's not just your decision. Have you discussed this with your husband?'

'Yes, I have.'

'And he agrees?'

'Please, no more questions, Bu.'

'You're being unreasonable!'

'He is, Bu. Not me.'

'Well then, it's not a final decision, is it? Not if you disagree?'

'He doesn't care, Bu. It's been a month since he's been home.'

'What? Why isn't he coming home? Does he have to travel for his job?'

'Sure. He's employed in the arms of another woman. He's gone and opened up a 'new branch'.'

'Oh my god! Oh my god!'

'It's fine, Bu. It's better if we split up.'

'No, no, no! That's a terrible idea! You can't split up! It's just a midlife crisis that men go through. It's perfectly normal! Your father went through it. So did Uncle Mursid, and Herry your favourite uncle too. Nearly every man under the sun likes the taste of another woman now and again. It's normal! Nothing wrong with that!'

'Wait, are you saying that while he's off having his escapades I should just pull myself together and carry on as normal?'

'Yes. That's what it takes to be a good wife. You must

learn to suffer. You learn to survive. Be strong! See? I'm strong! I'm still standing, aren't I? Your father can run around with whoever he likes, but I'll still be waiting for him. Right here.'

'But Bapak has never come back –'

'All I know is I'm still standing here, and I have you and your siblings.'

'I'm not you.'

'But you must learn to be like me. You must.'

'I don't think I can do this, Bu…'

'Stay strong. Until you die.'

'Bu…'

'You must. It's not for me. It's for your own good. You can't get divorced. That would only bring shame.'

'…'

'I'm your mother and I would never ask anything of you. I just want you to hang on in there and survive. Do it for me. You've always been my favourite. You don't want to upset me, do you? You don't want to be a disappointment, so I'm ashamed to look at my own daughter. So just do it for me, that's all. I've never asked you for anything. I don't see what the problem is… Tell me?'

'…'

Family Portrait

You're looking at our family portrait. Think you know who that is in the middle? You're right, it's me. I'd just graduated from junior high. Look at my hair, standing on end like the tufty bristles of a palm fibre broom. Did I have darker skin back then? Yes, I used to love playing out in the sun. But that was a long time ago. If you compared the paleness of my skin now to say, Mariana Renata's – well, if it were a competition, I'd win. The young boy standing next to me is Addo, my older brother: the most emotionless, unreadable guy in the world. Ibu always says he remindsed her of Kakek,[*] who was never much of a one for talking. Addo never utters a word unless it is absolutely essential. His interest in conversation has diminished over the years, reducing his sentences to monosyllabic utterances, just grunts and mumbling. But despite his social reserve, you can never doubt his intelligence. Whatever I set my mind to, I'm never a match for Addo's sharp intellect. His high IQ and sheer brainpower always put me in my place as the younger brother.

Standing on the right in the portrait is Kanya, my beloved sister. She's beautiful, isn't she? I was always so jealous of her. It was only natural: she was the only girl of us three siblings and always got her own way. Whatever she felt like, whatever she wanted, we had no choice but to do as she said, or she would burst into fits of tears. I can still

---

[*]   Kakek - grandpa

remember the face she always pulled, that poor innocent look in her eyes that not only made you feel guilty, but forced you to sob even louder than she did in remorse.

Ibu and Bapak's love for Kanya grew every time they looked at her. Kanya's beauty seemed to become ever more striking with every year. Sometimes I wondered if they'd forgotten they had two other children living in the house.

Then one day something happened that made their affections for her fade, and this shift reminded them once again of my existence. Revenge is sweet: I was so happy finally to be noticed and fussed over for a change. You're wondering why this happened? Stick with me and I'll tell you, as soon as I've finished introducing the rest of my wonderful family.

At the front of the portrait, there are two people sitting side by side. On the left is Ibu, my mother, undoubtedly the smartest person in our family. She made getting a doctoral degree look easy – and I'll bet no one else in Indonesia did it as young as her. She was the youngest head of department and the youngest dean in her Psychology faculty. She wrote over a thousand papers and was often invited to give seminars abroad – that's how brilliant she was. Next to her sits Bapak, now an old man, his hair completely white. He was also highly intelligent, except he had a habit of forgetting things. He worked as an examiner, but always forgot the time and date of exams, even though he'd taken care to note down the timetables, marking them on his calendars at home and at the office. The reason was always the same: he'd forgotten to check his calendar in the morning before starting work.

Wait, what were we talking about? Ah yes! I didn't finish telling you about what happened to alter Ibu and Bapak's love for Kanya. The change came with the arrival of Jarot, a tall, well-built guy with a six-pack, dark skin and big round eyes. He had a loud voice, and when he laughed the glass in the windows vibrated. His hair was thick and curly, but unfortunately he didn't let it sit naturally. Instead he took to applying an excessive amount of gel to flatten it down, though there were always a few strands that escaped, dry and curly and tousled by the breeze. You can see him in our family portrait here.

Ibu didn't pay too much attention when he first showed up. Kanya had lots of male friends who came to visit during the week, Monday to Friday in the living room, only leaving us alone on Saturday nights. Jarot was different though. He always came alone, every evening, and even again on Saturday nights, and showed no sign of leaving until Ibu deliberately cleared her throat or dropped a pan in the kitchen.

It had never bothered me before, but as Ibu's complaints grew louder, I began to see that something had changed in the house. Kanya never used to be back late from college, always coming home by 4pm. But since she met Jarot she was rarely home before the 6 o'clock news, sometimes much later. And when she did come back, she was never alone. The guy with the muscles and dark skin was always with her.

I asked Addo what he thought about it, but he just gave a half-hearted shrug and mumbled something inaudible. This was always his response to things. If it didn't involve him, he didn't care. I knew Kanya's love life wasn't my problem either, but Ibu had spiked my interest. I wondered whether Bapak, always so calm and wise, was aware of what was happening under his nose.

Not long after, an entire week went by where Kanya didn't stop crying: dark circles became a permanent fixture under her eyes. I wanted to ask her what was wrong, what had happened, though I knew it must have something to do with that big guy. Instead I held my tongue and kept out of her way. I'd learnt my lesson in the past: asking her such personal questions would only make her cry more.

Unfortunately, every time she started crying I ended up crying too. I'm pathetic. Her cloudy eyes were contagious and spread to Ibu. We had a whole week of cloudy eyes. I wondered how Bapak could remain so calm and relaxed in the midst of this, shuffling around the house and throwing me cryptic glances. What was going on?

The following week, after driving me to school, Bapak called me back as I jumped out of the car.

'I need you to come home a little earlier today,' he said, smiling. 'There's something we need to discuss.'

'May I know why?'

'Family meeting.'

'What about?'

'You know… About your sister. About Kanya.'

'Is there something wrong?'

'We'll talk later, ok? Your mother will explain everything. It's too much to discuss now. I don't want to ruin the surprise.' He waved a hand at me to go.

That night I had no idea what was going to happen next, but the dinner table was piled high with food: lontong, sambal goreng, opor, semur daging. Too much food for one mealtime. We ate in silence, Ibu, Bapak and Kanya taking small portions while Addo and I piled our plates high and set about devouring the feast.

The meal was going smoothly for once, though Ibu looked tense. Kanya kept sniffing, wiping her nose every five minutes. I didn't pay her much attention; I was done with all the crying. Addo was unresponsive as usual, giving only the occasional grunt between mouthfuls.

As I was finishing my second bowl of ronde,* Ibu tapped her glass with a fork. I guessed it was time for her speech.

'You can carry on eating, Dito,' Bapak said, touching my hand. I didn't tell him I had no intention of stopping.

'This is about...' Ibu cleared her throat. 'This is about Kanya. She...' Her words were swallowed up by sobs, at which Kanya burst into tears too.

Now it was Bapak's turn to clear his throat, though no words came. Addo mumbled something, his mouth still full of food. We stared at the three of them sat across from us, clueless about what was going on.

'Are you pregnant?' The words flew from my lips before I could stop them, my voice quiet but loud enough that everyone heard. A slice of lontong and red potato landed with a splat on my nose. Kanya's aim was good.

'What did you say?' she shouted angrily.

Ibu stared at me as Bapak choked, swallowing a mouthful of unchewed food.

---

*   Ronde - a dessert of glutinous rice balls in syrup

'Don't joke like that, Dito,' he said. 'Why would you think that? Your sister is going to get married.'

'Well… It's just that Ibu and Kanya have been crying all week. I thought… Getting married is good, right? Who are you going to marry?'

'Why all these questions? She's going to marry *him*, of course. What's his name… Jono?'

'His name is Jarot, Pak,' Kanya hissed. This was the big guy with the dark skin.

'Yes, yes, Jarot. I remember,' Bapak said. Hearing the name of her future son-in-law, Ibu burst into tears and began to cry hysterically. Kanya followed suit, the two women sobbing uncontrollably as they both ran out to their respective rooms. Bapak, Addo and I were left at the table with more questions than when we'd sat down. I exchanged glances with Addo, the two of us picking up our forks to resume eating.

The next day I approached Ibu as she worked in the garden. We talked a little about the exam I'd had that morning, before she sighed, laid down her shovel, and finally told me everything I wanted to know. It came down to this: Ibu didn't approve of Kanya marrying Jarot. She worried about how much older he was than my sister. She worried that he might not support Kanya in going on to study for her master's degree if he wanted her to settle down and have children. But what worried her most, and what I could scarcely believe, was that she didn't want to have grandchildren with dark skin!

'You know, Dito… The dark skin gene is so dominant.

There's a good chance your nieces and nephews will have dark skin like their father.'

They weren't even married yet. Why was she worrying about grandchildren? Though I kept my opinions to myself, not wanting her to hit me with her shovel.

Ever since that momentous evening of tears, Ibu became actively against men with dark skin. Perhaps she saw it as her last weapon with which to try and dissuade Kanya from marrying Jarot. Every time she saw a man with dark skin on TV or in the newspaper, she felt compelled to comment on his appearance. I couldn't understand what had happened to her progressive outlook and logical way of thinking. And yet now she was so focused on skin colour that nothing else seemed to matter. The wise and level-headed Ibu I knew had changed, all because of the man her daughter wished to marry.

Six months after that special family dinner, Kanya got married. It was a small ceremony held at our house, with only our two families in attendance. In the lead-up to the big day, Ibu pushed Jarot into trying a variety of different skin treatments. Moisturising baths, mud baths. Herbal bathing, flower bathing. A bath where he was scrubbed head to toe with sea stones, all in the hopes of making his skin somehow lighter. He suffered through a week of treatments, emerging at the end with skin that was smooth and baby-soft, but just as dark as before. Ibu failed to conceal her disappointment.

I have a niece now, called Lupi. She's tall and strong, with cute curly hair and big bright brown eyes. And her skin colour? You can see for yourself in the portrait. She's just like her father.

Ibu squealed with delight when Lupi was born. She could only sing her praises when she started to crawl. And when she began to say 'Nenek… Nenek…' Ibu cried sweet tears of joy. Lupi is her treasure. And Jarot? Oh, Ibu adores him now! She can rattle on for hours listing everything she loves about her son-in-law. Kanya can be such a princess, always wanting things her way. Ibu says he's the perfect man to help her grow out of her childish behaviour. It's funny: whenever we used to go swimming at the beach, Ibu used to slather herself in a thick coating of sun cream to ensure she wouldn't get any darker. But now she uses a special cream to make her skin look more bronzed, so she can look more like her Jarot.

But that's not the end of the story. There's another chapter. Addo found himself a girlfriend (which I will never understand, because how does he talk to her when he only communicates in grunts?) and, just as she did two years earlier, Ibu became sullen and irritable. We endured a long week of her dark mood and waterworks, before a special family dinner and… yes, you've guessed it. He's going to marry his girlfriend and they will start a family soon too.

Bapak told me that Ibu wasn't keen on Addo's girl-friend at first, because she had very light skin, almost as pale as a sheet of paper. Ibu was afraid her grandchildren would have…

I asked Kanya whether she knew about this, but she just smiled at me knowingly. I still don't understand.

About Us

Jakarta, 2nd May 1980

The ivory-coloured phone rings from beneath the stacks of papers that litter the table. It's not very loud. The volume is set to low so as not to disturb the others in the office, but the ringing still surprises them and makes them look up from their large white sketch pads.

'Hello?'

'It's me...'

'How did it go? Did you get the results?'

'Yes, I've got them. I didn't think it would be so fast. I only had to wait fifteen minutes.'

'And? Are you?'

'Mmm.'

'Jesus!'

'What? Are you disappointed?'

'No, not at all. It's just... I can't quite believe it. It doesn't seem real. Are you sure we can trust the clinic? I mean, is it 100% accurate?'

'Why? Do you think it's not your baby?'

'What? No, I didn't mean it like that. I mean, can we trust the results. Is there any chance they could have made a mistake? Like, could they have mixed up your results with someone else's?'

'Be honest. You don't seem too thrilled about this. You can tell me if you're annoyed that I'm pregnant. First you're questioning the clinic's credibility, then you're doubting their competence... There's no point trying to hide your feelings. I can tell what's going on in your head. If you don't want it, that's OK, we still have time to end it.'

'What are you talking about? That's bullshit. What makes you think I'm not happy about it? It came as a surprise, that's all. I just doubted the quality of the clinic – don't I have a right to do that? – because you told me how rundown it was. And this morning we agreed we must have made a mistake with the dates of your period. We thought we'd miscalculated. Remember the calendar the doctor gave you...'

'It doesn't matter. I know what you're really thinking. I just know. Don't worry, I'll go to the doctors tomorrow and ask for the injection. You don't have to feel awkward or anything.'

'I don't think you get what I'm saying...'

The dial-tone sounds as the line goes dead. She's hung up, the ivory phone still pressed against his ear, mouth still mid-sentence.

Midway down a narrow street, a white house sits snug in its narrow yard. There are ferns growing, asoka flowers and rose-apples coming into bloom either side of a slender footpath that winds through the gravel up to the front door. The streetlamp beyond the gate has already blinked on for the evening, the dim yellow glow just bright enough to make out the door number. Lamplight and the flicker of a TV spill out through a woven blind not pulled fully down, revealing two legs stretched out on the brick-red carpet.

'Don't get the injection tomorrow.'

'Why shouldn't I?'

'Because he, or she, has a right to live. Let it be.'

'I don't think that's what you really want.'

'Says who?'

'Anyone who overheard our conversation on the phone this morning for a start.'

'Ahh!'

'Am I right?'

'No, you're not. You always act like you know what I'm thinking and how I'll react... I'd be mad to think that! It's our baby! My baby! Don't I have a right to say I think we should have it? Why have we ruled that option out already? You misunderstood how I reacted. Why won't you talk to me?'

'I'm confused.'

'Are you scared?'

'No, not scared. Just confused.'

'What are you confused about? Our future together?'

'Yeah.'

'Oh, please don't cry. You'll distress the baby.'

'But we don't have anything. We're only renting this house. And it's too small for three people. I mean, where would we even put the baby when it's born? Plus we live too far out from the city centre, and we don't have a car. When I go into labour, how would we reach the hospital in time? I just can't see how any of it will work. It's such a mess.'

'We'll muddle through together. It could be fun.'

'Fun for who?'

'For both of us. We're creative thinkers. We've never

done anything the conventional way – why should we start now? Please don't cry.'

'I just don't see how we're going to be able to make it work. Formula milk is so expensive. And then there's the diapers, and paying the paediatrician… How are we going to afford all of that? Neither of us earns that kind of money. And I'm not brave enough to ask our parents for help. No way.'

'You're thinking back to when we got married and Ibu said that we weren't their responsibility anymore. That we had to provide for ourselves now.'

'Yes. And your mother was right. We never did ask them for help, did we?'

'I know, but now we have a baby on the way, don't you think we could somehow summon the courage to ask them for a hand?'

'We won't know until we try, I guess. But is it a risk we're willing to take?'

'You're just speculating'

'Hey, when did you get so pessimistic? We had nothing when we got married, but we agreed to build our lives together from scratch. There was almost nothing left in our bank account after we'd paid for all the admin and little parties in our home. But look at all of the furniture we have now. The bed, the TV, the chest of drawers. One by one we saved up and bought them. We did that. No one else. And we can do this now.'

'I don't care about having new things – we can always just wait. It's just this is something we've never had to face before. We've got so much to get ready in such a short space of time. And, like it or not, we'll need money. I expect I could go back to work after three months maternity leave, right? We'd need someone to help out though. Could we ask my mother? No, she's too busy. Not your mother. I think she's too old. We could get a nanny? But we don't have that kind of money to spare. If I wasn't going back to work for a year or two, do you think we could live off your salary alone? All three of us? Have you thought about any of this?'

'Look, why don't we just see what happens? I've been promised a pay rise at work in a couple of months' time. Who knows, it might be quite a big one. We can put the extra money I'm earning straight into our savings account. And with your work, why not quit after your three months of maternity leave and freelance from home like you used to do? You earned a lot more than me back then.'

'That was a long time ago. Is there really a future in freelance work? Will people still need someone like me? And how am I supposed to take care of a baby while I'm typing and working from home?'

'I'm not saying it'll be easy. But don't forget, I'll be here every step of the way. You won't have to do this alone. I promise to work hard so I can provide the best for you. And for our baby.'

'I'm just scared we won't be able to cope.'

'We won't know until we try. And remember, you don't have to do this alone. I'm right here with you. Whatever the future holds, we'll face it together. If it works out, then we can be thankful for that. If it doesn't, well then, we'll deal with whatever comes. Hey, hey, come on now, love! Where's your brave heart? You've always been up for an adventure, you were always much braver than me. You're usually the strong one, having to carry me. I need that tough spirit now. Please, don't give up already.'

'If it was just about the money, it wouldn't be a problem. I don't mind living simply. But when you bring children into it, that's a different matter. I don't want our child to have a hard life. I want them to be happy, and healthy, and have everything they need…'

'Of course. And we'll do our best to make that happen.'

'You seem so sure about all of this.'

'I am. I really believe we can make it work. Have you prayed about it? You once told me that He never tests a person more than they can handle, right? So please, stop crying now. Let's sleep. It's two in the morning already. Poor little baby will be an insomniac when it's born.'

Jakarta, 3rd May 1980

The small room is no longer dark. A king-sized bed is filled with two bodies wrapped around each other. A morning sunbeam falls upon an arm that is holding another body. An alarm clock is ticking from a side table. It shows 6:15. But the other clocks are showing different times: 8:15!

A pair of eyes is slowly opening. A lazy yawn. There is silence for a moment – then a scream.

'Oh my goodness! We're late! Wake up, honey! We're late!'

'Huh?'

'Wake up! Wake up! It's late! We've got to get to work!'

'What time is it?'

'See for yourself. I'm going to jump in the shower.'

'It's gone eight! How did we manage to sleep so late? There's no way I'll make it into the office on time. Maybe I'll stay home today.'

'You're going to call in sick?'

'Yeah, it's too late now. I might go to the doctor's for a check-up. I want to know how many weeks along I am.'

'Ah, that's exciting.'

'Do you want to come too?'

'Yeah, ok. As long as you don't mind?'

'Sure, if you think you can skip work. Let's go together.'

'I wouldn't miss it. Work can wait!'

The MetroMini speeds along, blowing up clouds of dirt from the road. Passengers cover their faces as the dusty haze drifts in through the windows.

'Poor little baby. Breathing in all the pollution.'

'We should buy a car, then.'

'We'll have to wait until we can afford one.'

'I wonder what the baby looks like.'

'Pretty weird, I expect. It can't be any bigger than a seed at the moment, right?'

'At four weeks? That's incredible.'

'Are you happy?'

'Yes, of course. Are you?'

'I'm not sure.'

'I'm so excited to have this baby. Just think, in a few months you're going to be a mother. Isn't that wonderful?'

'Mmm.'

Jakarta, 10th May 1980

She punches numbers into a phone. He answers after a couple of rings. A pen is moving around, pushing some numbers on the phone. After trying a couple of times, it works...

'Hello?'

'Oh, hey, it's you. Is everything ok?'

'I've got some news. I just got a huge, amazing promotion.'

'Oh wow. What level?'

'Five!'

'That is wild! Tell me everything!'

'I'm being promoted to sales promotion manager!'

'Oh my god! Who knew old Bruce had it in him? Finally Mr not-so-nice did something nice!'

'I was so nervous when I got called into his office, I thought there must have been a serious error in my sales plan. But it turns out he was really impressed by my analytics. He said it was time I proved what I could do as a manager. I was shaking. Honestly, all I did was compile the results of my research and pair it with customer experience, and then... and then...'

'I knew you could do it. My wife the superstar! Who'd have thought your literature degree could lead to you getting promoted to manager. We should go out for dinner to celebrate.'

'Great, but you're paying!'

'Since when was that the rule?'

'Since always. Besides, I won't get my raise for a while

yet. Quick, I've got to go. Mr Nice is coming over to talk to me. Will you pick me up later?'

'Sure. Give my love to your boss from the new manager's husband!'

'Will do. Bye.'

It's a café, not a restaurant. But a nice chill place to have coffee. Or fruit salad. Fancy cakes with tricky names. It's small. Quiet this evening. The waitress is standing by the door. Only one table in the window is filled.

'I have to go to the next regional meeting. It's in Hong Kong, I think.'

'How long for?'

'A week, max.'

'When is it?'

'In three weeks.'

'Does Bruce know you're pregnant?'

'Nope.'

'So what are you going to do? Can you still fly? The doctor said…'

'I know, I know. I have to watch I don't exhaust myself. And I shouldn't really fly long haul…'

'Can you do the training another time, say in a few months? Maybe the baby will be strong enough to travel then?'

'It's not that easy.'

'Why not ask Bruce?'

'Just leave it, ok? I couldn't ask that. He's promoted me to a really good position. I can't let him down.'

'They can make an exception for you, surely. It's not just

about modesty – it's about our baby. I'm just scared if you go then something will happen.'

'You worry too much.'

'Honey, listen to me. The doctor wasn't messing around. He didn't give you that medical advice just to scare you. He has a lot of experience with treating mums-to-be.'

'But what will my colleagues say if I ask him to make an exception? Rumours will start flying round the office. You know what they're like. They're all so jealous and two-faced. They hate it when Bruce praises someone, never mind promotes them. And there's no way I'm turning the promotion down. This is huge for me. I don't know if this kind of offer will come up again, not for a good few years at least.'

'I understand, but you need to think about what's best for the baby.'

'I am thinking about the baby. But I can't just forget about my career. Plus, you said yourself, back when we first got married and were thinking about children, you said it was important for me to stay in work and build a career. Don't you remember?'

'Yes, but I didn't say you should risk our child's life for it.'

'How can you say that? I have a good career ahead of me. This promotion will allow me to provide for all of our baby's needs. We won't have to lose sleep worrying about money anymore. That's why I don't want to let this promotion slip by. It's because I care about providing for our baby.'

'But I don't know. Maybe I'm just worrying over nothing. I'm just scared it'll harm the baby if you push yourself

too hard. It's not just the long training days, it's the travelling too. It'll be tiring.'

'I'll make sure I rest. I promise.'

'I'm just asking you to do what's best for the baby. Our
baby.'

'So you keep saying. Look, if something does happen
then maybe it wasn't meant to be. Not right now, anyway.'

'Why would you… What are you saying?'

'I don't know.

'I have a feeling…'

'What?'

'I just get the impression you don't really want to be a
mother.'

'Ah ha ha!'

'What's funny about that?'

'Sorry. Maybe you're right. I'm not desperate to be a
mum. At least not yet. I feel like a bullet, ready to shoot.
I know my goals, I have everything I need, and now I'm
ready to shoot. But once I pull the trigger, suddenly I'll
have to think about months of busy days. Breastfeeding.
It isn't easy. You know that, right? And our financial situation is so tight. Now my promotion has solved all of that.
I just don't want to lose it.'

'Even if it means sacrificing your baby?'

'Look, it's still early days. It's not like it's even aware of
anything yet. And even if it is, who knows, maybe it can
handle more than you give it credit for.'

'But even if the baby is strong enough, you could still
harm it if you overwork yourself.'

'We'll see.'

'I just want to see my baby born safe and healthy, that's all.'

'And to hell with my career?'

'It can wait. I know how clever you are. Your talent isn't going to go away just by missing out on one training week. Sit this one out and wait for another later on.'

'I'm not sure.'

'So?'

'I'm not going to let this opportunity slip by.'

'I didn't think you were this stubborn.'

'Maybe we both are.'

Jakarta, 12th June 1980

The television programme finishes. In five minutes or so, the TV will switch itself off automatically. A man lies across the floor in front of it, tired eyes gazing up at the ceiling, a sheet of fax paper crumpled in his hand.

'I lost the baby. Haemorrhage. Exhausted. My travel home has been postponed to 17th June. Please pick me up from the airport. Sorry.'

Jakarta, 24th January, 1985

The red car speeds down the road like a bullet, sound system blasting out *Act II Opening: Dance of the Swan* by Tchaikovsky.

'Dr Karno gave you bad news, didn't he?

'How did you know that?'

'You always put this on when it's bad news. You did exactly the same last time.'

'It wasn't deliberate.'

'So, tell me. What did he say? It's not good, is it?'

'I don't know. He said the test results were fine. You're healthy. And there's nothing wrong with me either.'

'So?'

'He couldn't understand why I can't get pregnant again. He said there must be something we're missing. He said we can have some more tests done, if we want, but not just yet. He said to come back in two or three months. The only thing he could prescribe was vitamins, just to make sure our bodies are getting what they need. Do you want to try them?'

'It's up to you. I'm willing to give anything a go.'

'You look so disheartened. Do you think we should just give up?'

'I'm not saying that, it's just – don't you get tired of it all? We've had all of the tests done. This must be what, the fifth time now? Every time you're sent home with the same results. Aren't you starting to doubt that doctor a little? He keeps drip-feeding us hope, all the while taking our money.'

'You're always so suspicious of people.'

'Can't he see that maybe it has something to do with your first miscarriage?'

'I don't want to talk about that.'

'I'm sorry, honey. I just can't help but wonder if it's related somehow.'

'I said to drop it! You want to know if I feel guilty? You

know I do. I've blamed myself for it for years. You don't need to remind me that it could all be connected.'

'I'm sorry. I'm so sorry. Hey, why are you crying? Please stop, we're at a red light. The other drivers will think something's the matter if you keep sobbing like this. Shh-hh, shhhh.'

Jakarta, 20th of July, 1991

The large bed is on the second floor of a large house. The tall glass windows stretch almost as high as the ceiling. There's an air conditioner inside the bedroom and in every room in the house. The sheer curtains, which can only be found in a certain exclusive shop, block the view. Two bodies lie side by side on the grey bed cover, staring up at the ceiling.

'I thought *Kindergarten Cop* would be funnier than that.'

'Yeah, the story's a bit simple.'

'But it would have been much cuter if they'd focussed more on the kids. Arnold could handle all the difficult situations. He was the one who had to fix everything. Maybe the director got too tired working with so many kids.'

'Maybe.'

'But those kids…'

'What about them?'

'They were so cute… I wanted to hug them all!'

'Mmmm.'

'If our baby had lived, how old would they be now, do you think? They'd be so cute, maybe already in school.'

'Mmm.'

'Maybe they'd be naughty. But smart like their mum, right?'

'Mmm.'

'Oh, you're asleep.'

And the bedroom falls silent.

The bodies lie with their backs to each other.

Suddenly the room feels so cold.

Far too cold.

24 x 60 x 60

Morning

'Darling, wake up please.'

'Hmmm…'

'Come on, it's already late.'

'Hmmm… Can't I sleep five more minutes, Bu?'

'No you can't.'

'I'm still sleepy, Bu.'

'I'm not surprised. You went to bed so late last night.'

'Is it okay if I don't have a shower, Bu?'

'No shower?'

'Yes, so I can use the shower time to sleep a bit more.'

'No way!'

'Why? Bapak will still be in the bathroom, right?'

'Bapak's not taking you to school today.'

'Oh. Is he working this afternoon instead?'

'Yes.'

'So you're driving me to school?'

'Yes.'

'Oh no.'

'What?'

'I should get up then or I really will be late. You drive
so slowly.'

'Oh, really?'

'Can I have a rose apple for breakfast, Bu?'

'No, you can't! I've already made your oatmeal.'

'How about tomorrow? Can I have a rose apple tomorrow?'

'No, stop being silly. Rose apple isn't for breakfast. Come on now, get up. You need a shower.'

'...'

(How annoying, stupid and maddening! Why didn't my alarm go off like it was meant to? Is that too much to ask from an alarm clock? Why did I have to wake up late today? Why has everyone in this house woken up late? Well, ok. Not everyone. Just me and my darling child. My husband, he's still snoring now. Sure, sure, sure, he got back so late last night. His last words were: You're taking the kid to school tomorrow. So picture the scene: now I'm frantically running around the house trying to get out the door on time, only to be reminded of my incompetence as a driver. It will be a miracle if I get him to school on time.)

Afternoon

'Hey.'

'Oh, hey.'

'What are you doing?'

'I'm having my lunch.'

'Did you collect him from school?'

'No, today is your turn, remember?'

'Yes, but I drove him this morning. So now it's your turn to pick him up.'

'Ah, yes, but I'm afraid I can't today.'

'Why not?'

'Because I'm at the restaurant.'

'Can't you just leave your food and finish it later? You need to collect our son.'

'No I can't. I'm in Pluit.'

'Pluit? That's so far away!'

'Yes, I'm trying a new seafood restaurant.'

'So, who's going to pick up Adi?'

'You are. It's your turn today.'

'I can't. I've got a meeting with a client.'

'Well why didn't you tell me that before?'

'I thought that...'

'Listen, he'll have to wait two hours if you want me to collect him. His school isn't anywhere near Pluit. But if you go and collect him, he'll only have to wait an hour.'

'So I'm the one who has to go and get him?'

'It makes sense, yes.'

'...'

'Hello? Hello? Hello?'

'...'

(This is so annoying! I'm so cross, I could scream. I want to throw my phone against the wall just to watch it break. I can't, though. It's my office phone. Plus, even if I smashed it into a thousand tiny plastic shards, it wouldn't change anything. I still have to go and collect our son. Our precious son who I do love really. Probably best to restrain myself. If I tore apart the office, they'd think I was having some kind of breakdown, that I'd completely lost the plot. They'd say it was too much for me, juggling my job with raising a child and keeping house. Failure, failure, failure! I feel like my head's about to

explode, though I've forced my lips into this fake smile I wear
at work. Stupid, stupid, stupid! And I still have to prepare my
presentation. I don't have time to drive over to Pasar Baru
to collect our son from school. But if I wait until after the
meeting's finished to go and get him, he'll overheat waiting
for me in that schoolyard. He'll have evaporated by the time
I get there! Argh, this is too much. I need to make a decision,
and quickly.)

'Hello, Mbak,[*] it's me.'

'Oh hi. How can I help you?'

'I just wanted to check, has this afternoon's meeting
been confirmed?'

'Yes, why?'

'Ah, it's just I think I'm going to be a bit late getting
there.'

'Oh. How late do you think you'll be?'

'About an hour…'

'Ah, but we have another meeting scheduled in an hour.'

'Could we push the meeting back to tomorrow, Mbak?'

'I'll see what I can do, but you know how much my boss
hates early morning meetings. Let's see… We've got a full
diary from noon until… Ah, we could fit it in at 4pm. Do
you want me to move it to then?'

'Can I quickly run it past my boss, Mbak?'

'Now?'

'Yes, right now. I'll be quick.'

(Come on, get a move on! I hurry down the corridor, waiting

---

[*]   Mbak - ma'am

for my boss to look up from her desk where she sits, biting her lip. I tell her the meeting has been pushed back to 4pm tomorrow. Oh, she says, raising her eyebrows. I think fast, telling her it was the client that asked for it to be moved. Liar, liar, liar! But I don't care, don't have time to care. I watch, waiting for what feels like years as she slowly opens up her diary, her eyes unhurriedly travelling down tomorrow's schedule. I'm glad no one's invented a heart-reader yet. I've no doubt it would capture my nervous palpitations, followed by a spike of sheer relief when she says she's free to meet tomorrow at four. Thank god: I thank her, dashing back to the phone. In five minutes, I'll be on the road to collect my son. Late, but I'll be there.)

'Hi, sweetie!'

'Hey, Bu!'

'What happened to your uniform? Why is it all wet and dirty?'

'I've been playing in the yard, Bu.'

'Have you eaten?'

'No, not yet.'

'Not yet?'

'You didn't give me my lunch money this morning.'

'Oh, sorry... Why didn't you remind me in the car?'

'I... I was too scared.'

'Scared? What were you scared of?'

'Umm... You looked fierce as a tiger on the drive to school this morning.'

'Ah...'

'Yes, Ibu! You should have seen your scowl in the mirror.'

'Ahhh!'

Evening

'Now that the meeting's been postponed till tomorrow, I want to run through our presentation again. There are some points I'd like us to clarify.'

'Sure. When would you like to go through it?'

'Now.'

'Now?'

'Yes, why not? Do you have another appointment?'

'Ah... No, I don't, Bu.'

'We can work on it in my office. Oh, and you can get the girl at reception to order in some pizza for your son. He must be hungry.'

'Okay, thanks.'

(There goes my hope of getting home on time, having a hot bath and going to bed early. The meeting went on till 10pm. My boy fell asleep on the couch. He slept in his uniform. I hope he didn't have any homework that needed doing. Or, if there was any, I hope he did it earlier when I was in the meeting. I hope he doesn't have any maths or social studies exams coming up. He's not great at those subjects. I hope his teachers have lots of meetings tomorrow. I hope there will be a day off tomorrow! I'm really hoping!)

Night

'Hey.'

'Did you guys only just get back?'

'Yes. Have you had dinner already?'

'Yes, I have. Have you?'

'Yep.'

'Okay, let's go to bed then.'

'We could chat for a while on the terrace, if you like?'

'Ah, not tonight. I'm really tired.'

'Oh?'

'Pluit was a long drive. I'm pretty sleepy now.'

'Oh, that's okay. We can talk in the morning, after you take Adi to school. We could go for coffee?'

'Hmm… How about the day after tomorrow?'

'What's wrong with tomorrow?'

'I have to go to Pulo Gadung tomorrow. It's quicker to drive there from here.'

'But I have to go to Surabaya the day after tomorrow. I won't be back until Monday.'

'Oh.'

'So, next week?'

'Hmm…'

'Oh, wait… If you're going to Pulo Gadung tomorrow, that means you're expecting me to take care of Adi all day again.'

'Hmm…'

'Honey?'

'…'

(So this man, my husband, is asleep already. I can't fall asleep until midnight. It'll be a new day in a couple of hours. There'll be a new set of tasks waiting to be done. When will it calm down at work? Why are the days going by so quickly? I suddenly feel so tired. I'm so sleepy. Maybe I should have a little nap.)

The Next Morning

'Dearest…'

'Hmmm…'

'It's gone 7 o'clock.'

'7 o'clock? Oh, I'm late!'

'It's not that late, sweetie. We could just decide that today will be a national holiday.'

'What!'

'Your son is jumping up and down. He's so happy that you're not up yet!'

'Why didn't you wake me?'

'Because you're the one who always wakes up early, sweetie.'

'…'

The Little One

'Let's take the little one home with us.'

'What little one?'

I didn't know who this 'little one' was, or why Nala, my husband, thought he needed to come home with us.

'Him!' said Nala, looking over at the small figure that sat leaning against the bridge's lattice railing.

The little one my husband was referring to was a boy of about ten years old. From a distance he looked like a regular healthy kid, but when you got closer you could see that something was wrong with his left leg, the sole of his foot twisted up at an odd angle. This wasn't the first time we'd seen him. In fact, we passed him most evenings on our way home from work, always sat in the same spot.

I became more aware of his existence after I saw Nala give him five hundred rupiah, and learned that he did this every day, every time we crossed the bridge from our office back to the car park where we left our car during the day.

'But why?' I felt like putting my hand to my husband's forehead – did he have a fever?

'For what it could mean for him, and for us. He could be our housekeeper. Or if not, we could still give him a better life.' Nala's argument was bold at best. How did he expect this kid, this young boy with a disability who couldn't even walk unaided, to play housekeeper? Our home was miles away from the city centre, a long walk from the nearest neighbour. My dear husband, how utterly adorable he could be; always going out of his way to ensure the happiness of others, to the point that he often forgot about his own happiness, about my happiness, ready to drop everything at his own expense.

But this time he'd gone too far. I had to do something to stop him, to change his mind, before it went any further.

'Well in that case we'll need more than one housekeeper,' I argued. 'Someone to feed him, to fetch him a drink when he's thirsty. Someone to help him get to the toilet.'

I could tell Nala was surprised to hear the firmness in my voice, but what did I care? He needed to remember that we weren't a charity; our home wasn't some humanitarian activist foundation able to take in every waif and stray he came across.

Nala stopped walking, just a few steps away from the boy, or should I say, our prospective housekeeper. Just like yesterday, the boy gazed calmly up at Nala from his usual spot. He didn't say a word, not so much as a thank you, as my generous husband carefully slotted his money into the empty mineral water bottle that sat at the boy's feet. All he did was grin.

I remember one afternoon I snapped, forbidding him to give any more money to his favourite person. 'Why do you keep giving money to such an ungrateful child?' I asked. Guess what he responded?

'Look at him, he's smiling!'

'What? That's not a smile! That's just his face, Nala! He can't close his lips because there is something wrong with his jaw. See, his teeth, his lips, they're not aligned properly. That's definitely not a smile, sweetheart!'

But Nala didn't listen. He had to follow his heart, continuing with his donations. As for me, I'd no desire to give the boy anything. It's not that I didn't feel for him. I just knew whatever cash the boy was given would be handed over to his boss at the end of the day.

I'd seen the man walk to where the little one sat on the bridge, collecting up the cash from the plastic bottle before glancing around to check no one was watching and hurrying away again. He did this at regular intervals throughout the day, returning once more at nightfall when he took the boy back home, wherever that might be. Nala didn't believe me when I told him what I'd seen, calling my story outrageous. But it was no less outrageous to let himself be manipulated and tricked out of thousands of rupiahs. Everyone knows that's how organised gangs of beggars make their money.

'So what?' said Nala. It's unbelievable how stubborn he could be.

I shook my head, attempting to drag him down the bridge after me. 'We can't decide anything right now. Why don't we sit down and discuss it properly later? There are lots of things we have to take into consideration. Come on, we need to get to the grocery store. We've run out of sugar and soap.' I felt his hand pulling me back. 'Nala, come on. That kid must have a family somewhere, I'm sure of it. Just think how they'll react when they come to collect him from the bridge and they can't find him. We'll be branded kidnappers!'

Nala didn't answer, but slowly his steps caught up with mine. I was thankful that, for the time being at least, I'd been able to change his mind, though I knew it wouldn't last forever.

He didn't say much as we walked down the road, nor at the grocery store. I could tell the little one was playing on his mind. I broke the silence when we got home. 'Okay, why is it that you so desperately want that kid to come and live with us?'

Nala was sat on the couch, about to watch television. He took a moment to think before answering. 'Look, maybe you're right. Maybe he is part of some beggar network. Maybe some man makes him sit alone on the bridge to beg each day with his foot on show, sore from where he's been forced to walk quickly across the hard ground. Last week, when you were off work with a migraine, I saw the man who must be in charge of the beggar network. He was yelling at the little one to hurry up and walk faster. And the boy was crying silently, hobbling down the stairs as best he could. I couldn't just stand by and watch. I yelled at the villain and told him to look after the boy. But he just glared at me. He said it was nothing to worry about, that he had it under control. He said the boy was nobody. If the bridge hadn't been so busy with people, I would have punched him in the face.'

I was speechless.

He continued: 'When the little one saw how angry I was, he started to wipe the tears from his face. He tried to give me his usual half-smile, but I'm sure I caught him giving a nod to the man, as if he'd been given an order to perk up, or else. He tried to hop down the stairs on his healthy leg, but he must have been in a lot of pain as he didn't get any further than the second step. Maybe he only did the one to prove to me that he was ok. It was like he was scared the man was going to beat him if he showed any sign of suffering. If this had happened on a Friday, I would have taken him home with me then and there. That's the truth of it, Mir,' he explained.

From the look in his eyes, I knew Nala had already made up his mind to go back for the boy. I had no choice but to agree with him.

'What about his parents?'

'He's better off without them. They're the ones profiting from him, exploiting his disability every day as a way to beg more money. He's probably the main source of the family's income.' Before I could open my mouth to speak, he started up again. 'Look at our house. It's easily big enough for three.'

For three? Suddenly this house could shelter three people, could it? Ironically, just a few months ago, when my mother asked if she could stay a couple of weeks, Nala had insisted the house was much too small for three people. 'The house feels crowded enough with just the two of us. Think how cramped it would be if your mother were to stay too, Mir. We'd be tripping over ourselves,' he'd argued at the time. How strange that now the house was big enough for three people after all. I couldn't stand it. I wanted nothing more than to shut him down, but when I thought about it, I decided that reminding him of his treatment of Ibu was perhaps not the best way to win him round. I needed another line of attack.

'Ok, say our house is big enough for us and the kid.

What about the rest? You wouldn't have time to take care of him. And I don't want you leaving it up to me either, you hear? Who'd look after him all day while we're at work? He's a human being, Nala, not a cat!'

'That's exactly why, Mir! Where's your sense of empathy?' Nala's voice grew louder.

'This isn't just about empathy! You have every right to feel compassion for the boy, but you need to think practically too. Just stop and think about it for a moment. How would it all work? Would you be able to go into the office later in the morning and then leave early to get back home to take care of him? I don't think so. And I couldn't either. We can't just leave him sitting in the corner while we go about our lives as normal. He needs to see a doctor and he probably needs some kind of walking aid too. Plus he'll have to go to school. What he needs, what we need – it would be too much. It wouldn't be fair on him. Sometimes, if you really want to help someone, you have to realise you might not be the solution.' I tried to soften my voice, keeping it free of the tension I felt.

Nala leaned back the couch, eyes fixed on the television. I hoped he'd taken in what I'd said.

'I'm tired.' He stood up abruptly and walked out, leaving me alone in the living room. I couldn't believe it. Nala never went to bed before midnight.

This was the second argument in our three years of marriage that had ended in Nala giving me the silent treatment. A year ago, Nala had taken himself off to bed early, just like tonight. That time it had been because I'd refused to go with him back to his hometown to visit his mother. I couldn't because I was still in the probationary period for a new job and couldn't risk making a bad impression by taking time off. But Nala was keen to go back home to celebrate his mother's birthday. I insisted I couldn't join him this time, reminding him that we'd only been at his mother's house in Solo that past month to celebrate Lebaran. He'd refused to see my side of things, stomping off to bed hours before his usual bedtime. It was two days before he'd spoken to me again. In those two days I'd relented, booking the time off work to travel back to his hometown with him to celebrate his mother's 61st birthday. My boss gave me a stern warning when I got back. When I told Nala, he assured me that next time he'd listen to my reasons. 'I promise,' he said.

Tonight I'd told him what I thought about his plans to adopt the little one, stating my reasons clearly. I knew he could see the truth in my argument, but instead of choosing to resolve the matter, he refused to back down, unwilling to consider a viewpoint other than his own. Maybe he hoped his silence would make me change my mind again. But it wasn't going to happen.

I could hear the cicadas chirring outside, in the cold silence of the night.

Morning

Nala woke early and was waiting for me in the kitchen when I came down. He set my breakfast on the table, kissing me on the cheek.

'I'm sorry about last night. Maybe you're right,' he

smiled.

My heart leapt. Of course I was right! I always am. Not that I said that to him of course. I just smiled and pulled him into a hug.

A week passed where nothing much happened. The little one sat in his spot on the bridge as usual. Nala continued to give him money, sometimes adding an apple or an orange or a slice of bread. I felt uneasy, though I kept it to myself. I watched in silence, curious as to what Nala's next move would be. Maybe he was working on a new strategy to change my mind. Just don't get your hopes up too much, dearest.

'Mir, will you do something for me while I'm away in Batam the next few days?' he asked one day, handing me a cheap sweater intended for his precious little one.

'You want me to give this to the kid?'

'Yes, would you, please? I thought he could do with a sweater now the rainy season's here. The wind's so strong these days, he must be cold.' He smiled at me sweetly and I said I would. That smile always melts my heart.

I'd be without Nala for two days, though he assured me that if anything urgent came up he could return by the next evening.

I left the car in our usual car park. It was a bit out of the way, but the monthly fee was much cheaper than for the office car park. Walking along the bridge, I saw the little one was wearing Nala's sweater. It was big on him, though I didn't think that mattered, so long as it was keeping out the cold. I hoped the generous Mr Nala wouldn't notice the little one's weight loss on his return, or he'd be carting the entire contents of our fridge out with him to the bridge.

As I drew closer, I remembered I didn't have any loose change with me. I took my purse out of the main pocket in my briefcase to look for a thousand rupiah note, but before I could find it someone hit me hard from behind, knocking my shoulder and snatching up my wallet. I screamed. People nearby turned around, including the owners of the market stalls selling keys and combs and gemblong cakes. They just stared, no one making a move to help.

I saw the pickpocket jump down the steps. I ran after him, trying to keep up though my heels slowed me down. I watched as some people on the ground tried to catch him, but the thief was getting away. I shivered, my legs and hands suddenly feeling the cold.

I called Nala when I got home that night and told him what had happened. He was quiet. I wanted to scream as loud as I could.

The next day I hurried up the steps to the bridge where it had happened. Three steps from the top, I noticed the little one already there, which was unusual given how early it was. You didn't make enough last night then, I thought to myself. He opened his mouth as I passed him, making an unpleasant groaning sound as he waved his hands, his eyes staring up into mine. What was he trying to say? I told him if he was asking for money, then sorry, but I was all out. His moans grew louder, one hand reaching to me while the other disappeared under his dirty sweater, as if searching for something.

Putting aside my annoyance, I approached him. He fumbled under his green, now grey, sweater and pulled out… my black purse! A few of the stitches had been torn, but still, it was my purse! I couldn't believe it, immediately crouching beside him to take it from his hand.

'Thank you! But where did you find it?' I asked him, my voice a whisper. I couldn't believe my purse had been returned to me. I sighed, already exhausted at the thought of sorting out replacement cards.

Nala's beloved little one attempted a smile, resulting in a grimace. With difficulty, he told me how he'd come across the purse. The pickpocket, in an attempt to shake off the people trying to catch him, had thrown the purse into the little one's lap. When night came and the pickpocket still hadn't returned to collect it, the little one decided to wait for me to walk by in the morning so he could return it safely to me himself. He asked me to check its contents. Looking inside, I saw my money was still there, as were all my important cards, notes and papers.

I'm not a sentimental person, not prone to soppy displays of emotion, but at that moment I reached out and hugged Nala's little one. I thanked him over and over as I fumbled through the notes in my purse, pressing ten thousand rupiah into his little hands. Suddenly I felt someone watching us. I stood up quickly, cutting our sentimental moment short. Realising I was going to be late for work, I headed off.

I called Nala as soon as I arrived at the office. His phone was off; he was on the flight home. I tried to focus on my work, but my thoughts kept wandering back to the little one on the bridge.

He'd sat out on the bridge all night in the hope of returning my purse to me. He could have just done his normal working day, then handed my purse over to the villain that controlled him, who probably took everything the boy earned anyway. Or he could have waited for the pickpocket to return and asked him to split the profits. Or he could easily have kept everything for himself.

I would never know what made the pickpocket throw my purse to the boy. What I did know was that he must have shivered through the long night, cold and hungry. For me, someone who'd never given him so much as a rupiah. What's more, someone who fervently discouraged her husband from his plans to help him. Maybe Nala was right after all and I was outrageous. I knew I had to do something to repay the little one. I left the office half an hour before I was due to go on my lunch break. I told my boss it was urgent, that I needed to go home and sort out my lost ID card and driving licence, along with everything else I'd lost with my purse. He believed me. I rushed into the elevator, my mind fixed firmly on my plan: I was going to bring the kid home.

After settling him at home, we'd look into taking him to a foundation for disabled children. We'd pay for everything he needed. We could do what was best for him and allow him to be a normal child, able to play with others his age. He wouldn't have to beg for money anymore. We could take him to a doctor for his leg too, and get them to look at his mouth and his difficulties with speech. At the very least, we could buy him a crutch or walking frame to help him get about more easily. I could get suggestions from Yayasan Melati. I'd heard their foundation had a special programme for children with additional needs.

The street outside the office was crowded; people were gathering round the bridge like something was going on. I tried to push my way up the steps but it wasn't easy. I started to worry that I wouldn't be able to find the little one after all. I decided to postpone my plan; I'd return after lunch when there were fewer people around.

Walking back down the steps, I paused to try and glean some information from the man selling papers. 'What's going on, Pak?'

'A little boy fell off the bridge,' he said flatly.

'A little boy? How did that happen? Where was his mother?' I asked. How irresponsible she was, I thought to myself.

'Not that kind of little boy. A beggar. A disabled kid. He usually sits down there on the bridge, but...'

No... I hoped I'd misunderstood. How could he have slipped and fallen? He knew the bridge so well. He'd been sat on it for months. He couldn't have just fallen off!

'But how did he...?' My head was spinning, my vision blurring as I tried to take in what the man was saying.

'It seems like someone pushed him. I don't know, he must be caught up in some kind of criminal...'

Stop! I could guess what had happened. The pickpocket had come back for my purse, and when the little one told him he'd given it back to its rightful owner, the pickpocket had gotten angry and...

My head was thumping, spinning so fast I could see stars. I felt my body tremble and I was falling...

The Trip

The train from Gambir to Yogyakarta is almost empty. She sits beside me, watching the children walk up the aisle trying to sell mineral water. A second later, she shakes her head, smiling. 'I love being on a quiet train. It's so calm,' she says, turning to me. 'We can read in peace, sleep without being disturbed, have a chat.'

'Gossip is good too,' I add.

She laughs softly, brushing aside her wavy hair, now streaked with grey. Something catches her eye in the seats to the left, across the aisle from ours. She stares for a moment before pretending to fix her shoes. I struggle to contain my laughter. Holding my breath, I cast a furtive glance in the same direction. Her sharp eyes were right. A young man stares keenly across at us, making no effort to conceal his gaze.

'You see?' she whispers, looking at me.

'He's staring at both of us, not just me.'

'Don't be ridiculous. As if an old woman like me could still draw such wide eyes from a man. Can't you see my grey hair?' she says, flicking the silver strands in my direction. We fall about laughing.

I feel a secret rush of pride. In my forties, married with a child, and yet I'm still charming enough to attract a man's attention. And a young man at that! The train starts to move. She's smiling, happiness in her bright eyes. This is an important trip for her.

'It's been a long time since I took a train. So long…'
She takes a deep breath.

'How does it feel?' I ask.

She turns and looks at me. 'I would have cancelled it, if I could.'

Her answer surprises me, my reaction prompting her on.

'But I couldn't. I have to get there as soon as possible. There's something I need to do.'

'It must be important.'

She nods. 'Yes, it's very important. I should have done it a long time ago. But I regret I never had the courage before. Maybe, I don't know… One minute I'd find the confidence, the next I'd have my doubts. But if I don't make myself go, it'll never be over. I can't… I can't avoid it any longer.'

'And now you feel brave enough?'

She nods, then stares out the window, continuing in a whisper. 'Everything's changed. The rice fields have been turned into factories. There are no wild stretches of land anymore. It's been a long time since I've travelled this way.'

I don't say anything; words feel unnecessary.

Her eyes rest on the horizon, gazing at the expanse of clear blue. A train attendant approaches us, offering a selection of drinks.

'A cup of tea, please,' she says. 'No sugar.' Once the attendant has gone, she whispers, 'It's embarrassing. I'm so sentimental this morning. Let's talk about something cheerier, shall we? I'm in need of a good chat right now. Something to make us laugh.'

I shrug, wracking my brain for something of interest to tell her. I only have stories about my daughter and all her needs, my struggle to balance my work and family life, how I'm missing my daughter, even though the journey's only just started. The end of the day looks so far away.

I'm sure she's doing just fine with her father. Ah yes… my husband. For some reason, he always seems to be related to my constant headaches. I find I'm forced to take myself off for walks, to go away on short breaks. Anything to avoid seeing him for a few days. I'm tired of watching him lie about the house, playing games on his computer. Back when the company he used to work for had a restructure and let some of their employees go, he was determined to use his severance pay to build his own company. Instead he was transformed into a lazy ass.

My mind explodes when I get home from work each day to find he hasn't given our daughter her bath, or even cooked her dinner. What the hell has he been doing all day? It's not like I can reduce my hours at work when it's my salary that's providing for our family. I don't know what happened to the man I used to adore, why all of a sudden he became such a leech, only getting up to move when his stomach rumbles. Where's his fighting spirit? The man I loved has disappeared.

And don't get me started on the stress of my daughter's school run. He knows I have to dash off to work in the morning, but instead of helping to get her ready he prefers to lounge in bed. His excuse is always the same: he went to bed too late the night before. I want to scream at him, but we're still living in my mother's house, so I can't. I have to put on a brave face. Every morning, every night, whenever we see each other, I have to look happy.

This trip is an escape from all that, a chance to get away and clear my mind. A day or two without my beloved husband will give me time to think about the future and what I want to do. Maybe. I really hope so. I take a deep breath in, slow and deliberate.

'I'm sorry if I made you gloomy,' she says, patting my knee. I shake my head and try hard to smile. I don't want to share my story. I know what she'd say to me: if you love him, stay with him. It's your life, your choice. But I'm not ready to talk about it. Not on a pleasant morning like this.

A train attendant with red lipstick is standing next to me, offering us steak and fried rice. My travel companion asks her directly, 'Is the steak cooked like before?'

The question takes the train attendant by surprise, her thin eyebrows shooting up so they're almost lost beneath her fringe. 'What do you mean, ma'am?' Answering her question with a question.

'The steak with semur sauce and empal…' my companion laughs, which makes me laugh too. The train attendant looks on in confusion, not knowing whether to smile or scowl.

'What I mean is, if the steak is cooked with the traditional Indonesian sauce like it used to be, then yes, I'd like to order it. But if it's cooked in the modern way, like it's served in restaurants nowadays, then I'd prefer nasi goreng instead, please.'

The train attendant's face lights up with a smile. 'Oh, the steak hasn't changed. It's like it's always been.' And so, finally, we order two portions of steak.

'Sometimes I wish I could go back to my childhood. Life seemed so simple. Everything looked beautiful,' she says. 'My parents were farmers, breeding cattle and horses. With their earnings, they managed to send me to Java for higher education. It was the first time I'd left our small island in the east of the country. Before I left for my first term, my father sat me down and told me that I needed to focus and study hard if I wanted to reach my goals. Once I'd finished my education, he wanted me to return to the farm to help grow the family business. I had eight brothers and sisters, each waiting for their turn to go and study in Java.'

'And did you?'

'To start with. I managed to find a job in a bookstore while I was at college. It didn't pay much, but it was enough to cover my college fees and living costs. It meant my father didn't need to send me money anymore.' She continues to gaze out of the window as she speaks. 'It was a struggle, balancing my studies and my job, but amid the busyness I met Juna. We'd been friends for a long time, but became closer during the last semester when we found ourselves in a lot of the same classes. My friends and I all thought he was cute. Smart, too. I couldn't stand how girls all over campus were obsessed with him. He loved me, I was sure of it, and my love for him only grew stronger. I was jealous of anyone who looked twice at him. But when I think about it now, love isn't supposed to be like that. When we first got together, I was so proud to have beaten my girlfriends who all wanted to be Juna's sweetheart. It felt good to have him all to myself, like I'd won. That fact he'd chosen me made me think I was somehow better than any of them… I was so arrogant.'

'And did you marry him in the end?'

'In a way.'

'In a way?' My voice reveals my curiosity and she turns to look at me.

'You're intrigued.'

'Yes, I am. But please, you don't have to tell me, not if it troubles you.'

'It doesn't trouble me. On the contrary, I feel I must tell you. Now is the right time. I only worry, are you ready to hear it?' She continues without waiting for my answer. 'I know this is the right time…'

The train attendant returns with her assistant, both of them carrying a Ktereta Api Indonesia tray with our meal set on it.

'Come on, let's eat it while it's still hot. It'll be tough as rubber if it gets cold,' she says, cutting her steak into pieces. She's right. The steak is already a little rubbery and takes me a while to chew. I think about her story, cut short by the arrival of the train attendant, and try to guess what happens next. I cast a glance in her direction. Her expression is neutral, though she seems pleased with her meal, mumbling to herself about the deliciousness of the steak.

'You look worried. What's wrong?' she asks.

I almost choke. 'Nothing, I'm fine,' I say, shaking my head.

'Ok, good. But if you have something you want to say, you can tell me. I always used to think that as women, we had to keep everything to ourselves, that it wasn't good to share our problems with others. I told myself that I couldn't bother anyone, couldn't involve them in my troubles. I was scared my problems would become public gossip; scared of the shame that would bring…'

'So we must share our stories then?'

'I think we must. When we share our problems with others, our hearts are unburdened and our walk becomes lighter.'

'But then everyone will know what's going on in our life.'

'So be it. Nobody's perfect. All we can do is try to be honest about our imperfections. We're all on a journey to becoming a better person.'

'But rumours could ruin our reputations, our family names… They could come back to bite us later on. They have the potential to destroy our careers. Honestly, it sounds dangerous, being so open like that.'

'Yes, it's not easy, that's for sure. But based on my experience, if we pretend to be okay when we're not, we only end up suffering more. We're always coming up with excuses, with cover stories, ready to lie anytime to save face. We're like professional liars. We have to lie a million times. Every time we're asked a question, we have to start from the beginning. Over and over, the web of lies gets bigger and bigger until we die. It's almost too late for me now. I should have been honest from the start. But better late than never, right? This time I'm going to tell the truth. The ugly reality of my personal life may shock people, but once I've shared it and it's out in the open, I'm sure I'll feel so much better. That's what I believe.'

'Is your story part of this?'

She nods her head in response. 'Juna. Arjuna was so charming. We were together for three years, or at least I thought we were together. I'm not sure he felt the same. We never had much time alone together. There always seemed to be a trail of girls following him around. They sent him so many gifts, and gave him long lingering hugs. I couldn't bear it, but when I lost my temper Juna told me I had to stop being so possessive. He said I needed to understand that being a broadcaster and writer while he was still a student attracted a lot of attention; he was popular among his friends. I had to learn to share him with other people. I tried to understand, tried to get used to his status on campus, but he didn't make it easy.

'Then one day Juna said he wanted to break up. I was so confused. I was lost without him. But I was also very bitter. My enviable status disappeared overnight. I had to accept that all those girlfriends who'd believed they just had to wait to get their chance with him had won. I was scared to face my parents, because I wrote about Juna all the time in my letters home to them. I'd even sent them a photo of the two of us. We were only hugging, but my father said our pose was too intimate for an unmarried couple. Back then, Javanese people didn't pose for photos together like that.

'They often asked me when we were going to get married. My answer was always, as soon as possible. I even told them that Juna would come to see them to ask for my hand, and that he'd propose to me soon after. But that was just my wishful thinking. In reality, I didn't hold out much hope for a proposal. The mere thought of engagement scared him to death. I don't know where I found the courage, but one day I took a chance and set a trap that would mean Juna would have to step up and take the plunge.'

'Step up?'

'I remember him staring at me, taking my trembling hands in his as I told him I was pregnant. It was the stupidest thing I've ever done. Back in high school, I had friends who went off the rails and found themselves pregnant before they'd finished their studies. I'd told my parents about them and promised I wouldn't make the same mistakes. Not ever. But what had I gone and done? In full knowledge of what I was doing, I threw caution to the wind and left all my ambitions behind.'

'What about Juna?'

'I asked him to marry me, but he refused. He said he wasn't ready. He asked me to wait a while, at least until we'd finished our studies. It wasn't that long, he said, just until the end of the year. But I didn't want to wait. Waiting meant my belly growing bigger, feeling ugly and embarrassed. It was then he suggested we abort the baby. I agreed to begin with, reminding myself that I didn't know the first thing about how to care for a baby. And it would mean I could continue with my studies. But something was pushing me to keep this baby. To make things worse, Juna had been avoiding me and it was difficult to pin him down so we could meet in person. On our last date, I'd succeeded in persuading him to marry me as soon as possible. We didn't need to throw a party, or even to tell anyone, I said. All that mattered was that our baby was born with legitimate status. He agreed. But the next day, when the papers had been prepared and the witnesses were assembled and ready, Juna didn't show up. When the Officer of Religious Affairs said he had another ceremony to get to, I couldn't control my tears. Suddenly, someone I knew very well arrived and took a seat in the empty chair beside me. The officer asked him curtly, 'Are you Arjuna Dwikara?' and the man sitting next to me nodded. I was about to scream when the man took hold of my hand, looking me in the eye as he said 'Sorry I was late.' At that moment I understood that I needed to stay silent. The ceremony went on without a hitch.'

'Who was he?'

'He walked me home after the ceremony. I kept quiet the whole way back, afraid to start up a conversation or ask one of the many questions buzzing around my mind. He held my hand. It felt warm. When we stopped in front of my apartment, he whispered 'You'd better know my real name. I am Semiaji Dwikara.' This took me by surprise. 'I'm Arjuna's brother,' he continued. 'I just returned from studying abroad. This morning, when I saw my brother set off with his rucksack, I knew he wasn't going to meet you. I don't know what made me come. My plan was just to let you know that Juna wouldn't be coming, that it was best if you moved on and forgot all about him. But when I saw you sitting alone at the front with that impatient officer, I found my legs walking me forward to take the seat beside you. The rest is a blur.'

She looks deep into my eyes. I try to avoid her gaze, but she takes my hands in her firm grip and I can't speak.

'Do you want to know what happened next?' I nod. Do I have a choice?

'I decided to continue with my college studies. Semiaji? Ah, he had other plans already. Two months after the ceremony, he married his fiancée. They're such a good couple. When I told my parents about my marriage and pregnancy, they were angry and disappointed. I'd completely rebelled against our tradition. For a start, our marriage hadn't begun with the traditional proposal ceremony. Ayah and Ibu wanted me to go home with Juna and our baby. Of course, I declined. I had the baby, but I didn't have a husband. I told them I couldn't go back home just yet, because the baby was still too young and Arjuna had been transferred to outside Java with work. They didn't send any more letters after that. I did try to contact them when the child was older. I wanted to introduce her to her grandparents, but I never received any word back.

'When I did receive news from them, it was a short letter sent from one of my brothers or sisters, acting as our go-between. The letters contained brief messages, telling me I had a new nephew, or that my grandmother had passed away. When Ayah died, I received only a telegram. The message read: *Ayah passed away last night. No need to come.* My mother had sent it. I cried a river of tears, not because she forbade me to return, but because I didn't have enough money to pay for the journey. I didn't care too much about what she'd said, about her ban. I just wanted to go home. I knew my mother would take comfort in my presence, and maybe in my daughter too. She'd need me there, and meeting my daughter would be a comfort to her.'

I feel the woman's hands in mine.

'Semiaji sent my daughter a birthday card every year until she was ten years old. On her eleventh birthday, Semiaji handed the task over to the person whose name he always signed on the card: Arjuna. The last time I'd heard from Arjuna was when my daughter was five. He'd said he wanted to start over, but I couldn't just forgive him, not after everything. The disappointment I'd felt the day he stood me up in front of the religious affairs officer still burned bitter inside me. Then when she was ten Semiaji came to meet me. He told me Arjuna wanted to start writing letters to his daughter. I didn't agree at first, but after thinking it over, I realised that maybe my daughter would benefit from a father figure in her life. And so, Arjuna began to write his letters. Fortunately, since Semiaji had always signed his birthday cards with Arjuna's name, when the real-life correspondent changed my daughter never knew. I remember her telling me once that the recent letters she'd received from her father had become so sentimental.'

The woman takes a deep breath and stares into my eyes. 'I made a lot of mistakes over the years, trying to keep my child from her father. I was so angry with him, so distraught by the way he'd treated me.' Her jaw stiffens, making her cheeks ripple. 'I was worried my daughter would go looking for her father one day, so I came up with a plan. I forced Semiaji to send a fake telegram with news of Arjuna's death.' My hands are cold and sweaty in her grip.

'But he was still alive?' My voice is strained.

'Yes, he's still alive. Alone. Unmarried. He said he

wanted me and my daughter to be a part of his life. I didn't believe him. Why would Arjuna, a playboy with thousands of women to choose from, end up alone without a partner? Why would he wait for me, the woman he abandoned on our wedding day? For all I know, he's still waiting. He'll be an old man now, no beautiful women trying to snap him up anymore. All his old admirers will have found themselves proper gentlemen to settle down with, not a Don Juan like Arjuna. I'm sorry to tell you all this,' she says, her voice softening. 'I get carried away with emotion. And this was supposed to be a nice trip for you, wasn't it?'

I choose not to answer her question.

'I'm ruining this trip with my story, but I had to tell you. It's not good to hold on to anger. I'm only going to get more grey hair and wrinkles; I don't have much time left, and bitterness won't help. I need to leave the past behind and forgive Arjuna for all the pain he's caused me in life. Maybe he really is remorseful and wants to do the right thing before it's too late. Maybe he simply wants to get to know his daughter.'

'But today…' I find I can't go on. My throat is sore, my hands clammy.

'Today I am taking my daughter to meet her father, Arjuna,' she says, looking deep into my eyes.

'But why?'

'I can't lie anymore. I'm just an old woman, but I'm also a mother. If I don't tell the truth and teach my daughter to be honest, then who will? I always wanted my daughter to be honest with me, to feel like she could tell me anything. But how can I expect her to share her worries and troubles with me if I'm not honest with her in return. I have to tell the truth. I know what it's like to go through life weighed down by a burden you feel you have to keep under wraps. Always pretending everything is fine, when deep inside your heart is broken and you feel like you're about to explode, like it's too much for you to carry. I don't want my daughter to keep such sorrow bottled up inside, to feel like she doesn't have a friend to talk to…' She takes a deep breath and continues. 'I hope that, after this trip, she'll feel she can share anything with me.'

She looks into my eyes, searching for an answer, but I don't know what to say. The train has left Cirebon, passing into central Java.

'So this is the reason for our trip?' I hear the words leave my mouth. She nods, her face tired. The judder of the train down the track is increasingly comforting. Slowly, I prise my hands from her grasp and hold her in my arms.

'Arjuna is ill. Seriously ill. He asked me to bring you to meet him. He really wants to see you,' she whispers through her tears. Out of the corner of my eye, I glimpse a young boy in the seat behind us. He stares at us, eyes wide, as the train continues to cradle us. In a few hours, we will arrive in Yogyakarta, where I'll meet my father. The train rattles on. The woman beside me, my mother, sits enfolded in my arms. The next half of our trip is waiting.

Baby

The moment the car door opens, the cry hits my ears. I tell you what I can hear.

'A cry? What cry?' you ask, tilting your head, trying to make it out. I insist you listen more carefully, but you still say you can't hear anything. We go inside. Turn on the lights. Shower. Sit down opposite one another in the living room. And I swear to you, I can still hear crying. Screaming.

We sit facing each other. You turn on the radio then start reading the paper; you don't like to watch too much TV. I sip a cup of hot tea. But the cry is still bothering me. I tell you again: that crying's getting louder. You stop reading for a moment, cock an ear, shake your head.

'I can't hear anything,' you say. I get up from the couch and turn down the volume on the radio.

'Can you hear it now?'

You close your eyes. After a moment, you open your mouth and say, 'Yes, faintly.' Then you go straight back to your reading. To me though, it only seems to be getting louder. Piercing. My head is aching. Maybe I just need to go to bed. But the cry follows me. You follow me. Lying down next to me, your breath warms my ear.

'I can still hear it,' I whisper.

'Just ignore it. It'll stop soon,' you say.

But it gets louder. It sounds like a cry of pain, I tell you. You start muttering again, insisting it'll stop soon. Your breaths become more even; you fall asleep.

The crying continues.

Morning comes, and the crying is still there. It's louder. Now you say you can hear it clearly.

'It's a baby.'

'A tiny baby,' I say. I'm worried about the baby.

'Don't be getting involved in other people's drama,' you say. I tell you it's not a question of drama, I just think the baby has been crying for a long time. I'm worried.

'Maybe he's just sick. Just like us adults get sick,' you say. I say if that's true, he needs to see a doctor and get some medicine. He's been screaming for such a long time. You let out a heavy sigh, starting to lose your patience. 'We could take him to a doctor and the doctor will give him medicine. But it just sounds like this baby's too pampered and always wants to be held. Too whingey.'

'Too whingey? A baby's only whingey if it's sick.'

'Says who?'

'Says me.'

You raise your eyebrows, curl your lip. I can tell you don't agree with me. But I know it. I can feel it. Before you even open your mouth to speak, I know what's going on in your head. You say you don't know anything about babies, because I'm still yet to give you one. No sign of a baby coming anytime soon, so how am I suddenly such an expert on a baby's cry? But in your heart, I know you know I'm right.

When you came home last night, I was ready to go straight to sleep. You sat down on the corner of our bed. 'I can still hear the baby crying. And it is late.' I kept silent. 'Maybe you're right and there is something wrong with the baby...' I kept silent, closing my eyes.

This morning I tell you to go to work on your own. I'm not going in. I'm going to visit the baby instead. I'll go to the pharmacy first to buy telon oil, baby powder and other things. I have to go, I tell you.

'No way,' you say, raising your voice.

'Why not? I have to go. I want to see that little baby. There must be something wrong with him. I'm afraid he's ill, or hurt. Those screams sounded like he was hurt,' I say. I know it. You shake your head, your forehead creasing, showing your disagreement.

'That baby's been screaming for too long!'

'I know, but don't go now. How about this evening, after work? We can go then,' you say.

'Both of us?'

'Yes, both of us. We can take some snacks for his mother. We can take… whatever you like. But let's go together.'

'Why do we have to go together?'

'So his mother isn't suspicious about your interest in the baby.'

I want to go now, really. Though maybe you're right and we should go together.

But then you come home very late. Almost midnight. I'm sure you did it on purpose. It's so late there's no way we can visit the baby's home tonight. You never intended to. Your suggestion of going together was just an attempt to delay our visit. I know it.

'The traffic was really bad. And I got a puncture!' you say.

'The traffic is always bad, surely you know to expect that by now. And a flat tyre?'

Your face turns red. 'I'm tired!' you shout, striding out of the room and slamming the door behind you.

'Are you tired of lying?' I yell after you. That wailing. That baby's cry. It hurts my ears. My head feels ready to explode.

'The baby's scream is getting so much louder. He must be in pain…'

You put on your clothes and get ready for work. I keep quiet.

You place a hand on my shoulder. 'I'm sure the baby's mother will have taken him to see a doctor. If he's still crying, maybe the medicine hasn't taken effect yet. Give it time. I'm sure the crying will stop soon enough.' I stay silent.

You hurry home that afternoon. 'I came straight home today so I could go with you to visit our neighbours, remember? Come on, then!' You seem enthusiastic. You're holding a bag full of oranges in one hand, and a bag of small packets of various sizes in the other. 'Baby gear,' you say, smiling as you hand the bundle to me, 'There's baby powder, telon oil, disposable diapers…'

'Don't bother.'

'Come on! There's no need to be like that. Get changed and we can go over there now.'

'We don't need to go round anymore,' I tell you. 'The baby's stopped crying now.'

You smile with relief, stroking your chest and placing a hand on my shoulder. 'Ah! Thank goodness!'

And then I tell you everything: that ten minutes before you got home, the chief of the neighbours' association knocked on the door to say a baby had died. Just before the Asr Prayer. They found his body covered in bruises and wounds. Beaten by his mother. She's being questioned down at the police station. I go into the kitchen, leaving you alone. Your smile is gone.

Son-In-Law

December 1993

'So, you seem all set on marrying this Javanese guy?'

'Yes.'

'His skin is quite dark, isn't it?'

'That doesn't matter.'

'You will have dark children.'

'That doesn't matter.'

'His traditions will be very different from our family's traditions.'

'I guess so.'

'To be honest, I'd be happier if you were marrying a man like your father.'

'You mean Chinese?'

'Yes, they seem so clever.'

'I didn't find one who stole my heart.'

'There wasn't anyone you connected with? Did you even look? Do you remember Pak's friend's son who came here the other day? He is so smart. Graduated overseas. He's such a blessing.'

'I just didn't like him.'

'What did you dislike about him?'

'Everything about him! His stiff hair. His oily face. His whitish skin reminded me of a gecko's belly.'

'Ah! So it's about his appearance!'

'And when I tried to have a conversation with him, he

didn't talk about anything other than his business. He wasn't interested in anything else.'

'Idiot! That's the most important thing! He's so intelligent, he's sure to make lots of money. He'd keep you and your children well fed. His parents are kind too.'

'He's too Chinese for me.'

'So, what's wrong with that?'

'That's exactly what I don't want. Just like Pak's family.'

'What do you mean?'

'Just that… People like him always think they're better than us. He probably thinks I'm okay to have as just a friend, but not a girlfriend. Let alone a wife! As if I'm looking for that kind of drama.'

'You're making this up. Your father never acted that way!'

'This isn't about Pak, Mak.* This is about his friend's son.'

'Why have you become so prejudiced?'

'I'm just stating the facts. I once heard his mum say she wanted him to marry a girl the same race as him. It's better, she said.'

'Ah…'

'They're just the same as Pak's family, Mak.'

'What do you mean?'

'Did you forget how badly Pak's older sister treated you? Every time we went to their house, she never even talked to you. And then their kids, they never invited us to play with them. Do you remember Pak's older brother?'

---

*   Mak - mother

Has he ever invited us to come to his house? And how about Pak's cousin who always spoke Hokkien when we were there?'

'That's all just coincidence.'

'Just admit it, Mak... Have you forgotten the time we met them all in Pasar Baru? They acted like they didn't see us. And when we pushed through the crowds to get closer and say hello, none of them smiled at us in return. Our hands were left in the air because they wouldn't shake them.'

'...'

'Mak, I really don't want to have any more to do with Chinese people like that. I'm so tired of being called a mixed kid, an impure kid. Am I petrol?'

'Do you blame me for marrying a Chinese man? Does having a Chinese father bother you?'

'It did once. But... it's kind of strange being a mixed kid.'

'Strange?'

'Yes. When I was in elementary school, my friends were all Chinese. And when they asked me what race I was, I told them I was Chinese. But they didn't believe me. They asked why I had such dark skin if I was Chinese. When you guys came to school to collect my report card, they told me I was indigenous. From then on, they stopped inviting me to play with them. When I was in junior high school, where there were no Chinese kids at all, my new friends asked me what my race was. I told them I was from Timor but they didn't believe me, thanks to these eyes. When you both came to school, they called me Chinese. They never spoke to me again after that.'

'Why didn't you tell me? That's so racist! I could have reported it to the principal!'

'Ah, but if they'd have found out that I'd told you, they would have made my life more difficult. It wasn't a big deal. What we should do is tell Pak and his siblings about my choice of husband, as a kind of payback...'

'So that's the reason you don't want to marry anyone Chinese?'

'Not really. I want to marry this Javanese man because he's never asked what race we are. He accepts me the way I am. He accepts my family too. That's all I need, Mak.'

'Do you regret being a mixed child?'

'Not exactly. I just want to have a different life to yours.'

'Honey, whoever you choose to marry, you'll come up against the same obstacles.'

'What do you mean?'

'Like it or not, by marrying him, you're also marrying his family.'

'Yes, I know that.'

'Good. So, are you sure you want to marry this Javanese guy?'

'Yes.'

'...'

April, 1996

'Your sister's getting married.'

'To who?'

'The boy from Bandung. Who else?'

'Oh, she is? That's brilliant.'

'Do you agree with her choice?'

'Yeah. You've finally got your wish of having a Chinese son-in-law.'

'Don't spoil things.'

'Who's spoiling things? It's the truth, Mak!'

'You've become such a smart-talker since you married that Javanese man.'

'Ah, this has nothing to do with him. I'm just thinking back to that chat we had before I got married.'

'Which one?'

'When you said you'd prefer to have a Chinese son-in-law rather than a Javanese one.'

'Oh, that.'

'Yes, 'that'.'

'...'

'Why? Don't you like your future son-in-law?'

'Your sister's boyfriend is so gentle, but...'

'But?'

'His parents...'

'What about them?'

'They're so arrogant. They never want to come here. Have they forgotten that their child is a boy? It's never been the tradition in our family for the girl's side of the family to visit the boy's side of the family first. Is that too complicated to understand?'

'...'

'Why are you so quiet? Do you agree with them?'

'Nope. But I'm sure they must have a good reason for not coming here. For now, at least. Maybe they're just busy.'

'No way. They're both traders who can travel as much as

they want, anywhere, anytime. They don't have a reason to postpone their visit to our house.'

'…'

'I don't like it when you don't say anything…'

'I'm just thinking.'

'Now's not the time to think. Now's the time to feel. I feel worried about…'

'About what?'

'That his parents don't fully agree with him choosing to marry your sister.'

'Ah, but they've known her for a good four years now. If they didn't like her, they could have said so before. Why leave it until now, when the two lovebirds want to get married?'

'That's just it!'

'What's just it, Mak? What do you mean? I don't understand.'

'Your sister told me their attitude towards her changed after she and their son announced they wanted to get married.'

'Changed? How?'

'They became very unfriendly towards your sister.'

'Hmmmm.'

'Hmmm, hmmmm… What are you trying to say?'

'Maybe they didn't realise their son was so serious about the relationship. Maybe they hoped he'd end up marrying another girl.'

'What do you mean?'

'I don't want to discuss this.'

'Why?'

'I think you know what I'm talking about.'
'…'
'I know you know, Mak.'
'Oh you…'
'Mak, stop it, just stop this!'

November 1999

'Hello, where are you now?'

'At home.'

'Your sister is due to arrive any minute.'

'Okay.'

'Maybe she'll stay at your place.'

'Ok, sure.'

'Maybe till next week.'

'Sure, she can stay as long as she wants. But why?'

'She can tell you herself.'

'Ah, what's happened, Mak?'

'Your sister had a fight with her parents-in-law.'

'Oh, why should she be the one to leave her house? It must have been a pretty big fight. What was it about?'

'Her parents-in-law want grandchildren soon, but she's not in any hurry.'

'But that doesn't mean she doesn't want to have a baby, right? What's the big deal if they have to wait a year or so?'

'Her parents-in-law say next year is a good year to have a child.'

'Why?'

'It's the year of the Golden Dragon, which is a good year to bear a child, especially a boy.'

'Oh my god… Is that it? Is that the big problem?'

'*Just* that? They've been fighting about it every day. And when things kicked off again this morning, your sister couldn't handle it. She decided to run away from her parents-in-law's house. Please, you must do something for her!'

'Ah, she already knows what to do!'

'What?'

'Just agree with them. Simple.'

'But she doesn't want to! She can't do it!'

'What an idiot. She has to do it, Mak!'

'That's easy for you to say, hmm? Can you imagine being in her position?'

'I'd agree.'

'You only say that because you're not the one married to him.'

'When she decided to marry that Bandung boy, she must have already known what she was getting herself into. If it's only just causing her a headache now, there must be something wrong with her. You told me yourself, whoever we chose to marry, we'd meet the same obstacles.'

'…'

'Mak…'

'You!'

'Mak, just get over it. Stop this.'

Taxi

The drizzling rain always causes traffic jams in Jakarta. Especially at this time of day, the post-work rush hour. The buses and cars steadily increase in number. It's hard to weave through the gridlock. I turn off the air conditioning; I try to save on gas. The rain doesn't bother me too much. Crowds of workers stand at the roadside. They're waiting for public transport, an affordable and comfortable way to get home. I hope one of them will choose my taxi. At the end of Jalan Thamrin, I spot a hand waving in my direction. There's nowhere to pull over so I slow the car to a crawl, getting as close as I can. My passenger is a woman. She breaks into an easy sprint to catch me; from her speed, I guess she must be around the same age as my older sister, Yuni. Slim with a short haircut. She throws open the car door and slides onto the backseat.

'Good evening,' I greet her. She's muttering as she checks the door is locked and tells me where to go: the east of Jakarta. I breathe a sigh of relief. I'm glad she didn't say the chaotic south of Jakarta, which is well known for its awful traffic jams.

From the rearview mirror, I study her face. She wrinkles her forehead. Maybe she's tired of the traffic jam already. I ask if she has a preferred route.

'Whichever you choose. I just want to get home as soon as possible. My kids will be waiting for me,' she answers, without looking up.

'Okay, we can just go down Imam Bonjol Street, Mbak...' I say.

'The traffic's always bad when it's raining, isn't it?'

'Almost every evening, Mbak,' I say.

'Too many cars in Jakarta.'

'Many rich people here, Mbak.'

She laughs. 'But many people still prefer to travel by taxi. Look how many people are waving their hands trying to hail a cab. And it's like this every night!' she says, pointing to a group of people all scrambling for the same free taxi.

'Ah, but it's only like this in the evenings and early mornings. And only at the start of the month. There are never any passengers in the afternoons. And if there are, they're never wanting to go far. It's just a stand-in for the bajaj* they usually take. It can be exhausting, getting up to be ready at the taxi rank for 4 o'clock in the morning while everyone else is still asleep. Luckily I have a motorcycle, so I don't have to leave too early. If I had to take public transport, I don't know when I'd get time to sleep. Or where I'd find the money to pay the fare!'

'Why do you have to be there so early?'

'Because we have to clean and check everything over. The sooner we're ready, the more likely we'll get lucky in collecting passengers from the airport.'

She smiles. 'Have you been a taxi driver for long?'

'I started last month.'

She looks surprised. Maybe she's not keen on being driven by someone new to the job.

---

*　　　Bajaj - a three-wheeled scooter

'What did you do before?'

'This is my first job. I was studying before.'

'What did you major in?'

'Computer science.'

'Where did you study? Was it a special computing school?'

'In Depok, at the Computer Academy.'

'Wow, that's great! Do you plan to continue your studies at university?'

I smile. 'No, I had to stop.'

'Oh, why? That's a shame…'

'Yes, I really wanted to keep studying and graduate, get a good job and earn a good salary. A different life than this. It's so tiring… But what can I do, Mbak? I have to forget any dreams I had. My family is counting on me.' I feel my voice trembling.

'You have a wife and children? You're married already? Oh my gosh, you look so young…'

From the rear-view mirror, I catch her staring at me with wide eyes. She doesn't believe me. My heart beats fast in my chest. 'I went straight to university after finishing high school. But three months into my studies, I discovered I was going to be a father.'

She listens as I pour out my story.

'Everything seemed great at the time. I was at university, while working a part-time job on the side. I thought maybe I could offer private lessons to elementary and junior high students. So did my wife. But when it came down to it, I had trouble finding students who wanted private lessons. Parents nowadays are so choosy about tutors for their children. With only my high school diploma, I had no chance. For a while I tried applying for jobs in garages, but they weren't interested. They don't want part-time workers because it makes things difficult when managing the salaries. What was I supposed to do? Fortunately, our new neighbour, who'd just moved in, came to the rescue. He told me about a taxi company who were looking to hire a new driver. So I passed the test and became a taxi driver.'

'What did your parents say?'

'They don't know about any of it. Maybe it's better that way. I didn't like how they belittled us all the time. I'd had enough of them. They didn't agree with our marriage. And they didn't care when I told them I wanted to stay at university and have a part-time job. They said I was too much of a dreamer. When I told them I was willing to do anything to earn money, they didn't show any concern at all. They said I'd made too many promises I hadn't kept. That I'd thrown away too many opportunities, with no sign of remorse. My wife lost all hope. We couldn't expect anything from them. We have to choose our own path now, whatever that might be. We'll do the best we can.

'It wasn't easy at the beginning. Things seemed impossible. I worried that if I failed to make it as a taxi driver, I wouldn't be able to pay the medical bills if our baby had to stay longer in the hospital. If I'm honest, every time I see my friends in the street, or the college students waiting at the bus station, I feel like I've failed. But when I remember my cute little children, and my wife, panicking as she cooks the rice, suddenly I feel better. The rice can be overcooked, it can be a porridge, it can be all dried out… the ratio of water to rice varies from day to day. It's so funny!'

My passenger laughs along with me.

'Sometimes I get annoyed when I see her re-reading her old magazines, gazing at those fashion pages. I feel like she's asking me to buy her new magazines, but I can't. I don't have the money. When I find her crying, it gives me a headache, which the little one makes worse with his own cries. I know she'd like to own some designer clothes. She's still young. But I can't give her any of that. Where is the money supposed to come from? I don't want to make unrealistic promises. What's important is that every day I can buy a bottle of milk. That's enough for now. My wife seems more settled recently. She seems wiser too. That puts my mind at ease.'

'Have you thought about going back to see your parents?'

'I always planned to, but they would come out with their stupid comments, mocking us. I can't take such a drain on my emotions right now. Maybe in the future, if my son can master peeing in a sling. Then when his grandpa holds him in his arms, he can take revenge. And when my wife has forgotten the cynical look on their faces. We're not ready to face them yet.'

As I'm sharing my story, my passenger seems pensive. She stares out the window.

'Do you drive every day?'

'Yes, Mbak.'

'Until what time? I mean, nights too?'

'Most days I work till midnight. But if I'm really exhausted, then I'll go home earlier. It's hardest when I get sick. Instead of using our money to buy a bottle of milk, we have to spend it on medicine.'

'Of course... we do everything for our children.'

'Yes, no matter how tired I am, no matter how frustrated I am with my situation, all those feelings disappear when I see my baby.'

'So, will you be driving until midnight tonight?'

'I'm not sure yet. I'm contracted to work until midnight, but sometimes I go home a little before then.'

'I guess if you earn enough money earlier on, there's no point in staying out on the roads.'

'It's not always about money. I have to take care of myself, to make sure I'm not getting sick. When I can feel my body aching and my eyes getting heavy, I know I'd better head home. Otherwise I'll end up spending all the money I earn on medicine. That's no good.'

It takes a moment before we realise we've arrived. It's a small house overlooking a garden with a play area, from which lively sounds emerge over the fence.

'That's my kid,' she whispers. I try to catch a glimpse but the gate is shut and the pickets are set close together. 'I really hope you make lots of money tonight, so you can take some time off to enjoy quality time with your kids.' She pats my shoulder and we laugh together once more. Handing me the taxi fare, she says she hopes to meet me again someday. I drive off slowly. I hear the clang of the gate closing shut. Another journey, another story. I'm quite confident my passenger believed what I said. The proof is in the generous tip I received. It's much bigger than I'd expected. Perhaps my high school Bahasa Indonesian teacher was right, and I'd do well to pursue my talent for storytelling. My stories were always convincing. She'd suggested I major in literature. Who knows, maybe there's a publisher looking for a young writer like me.

I feel guilty, but also pretty amused.

I look at the beautiful, clear sky. Next week, the actual driver will be back at work, and I'll go back to my real life and my prestigious university. If you were one of my passengers, I'm sorry. I was just trying to make as much money as I could to pay my fees. Maybe someday we'll meet again, though you may not remember the beautifully sad stories that touched your hearts. Forgive me. Goodnight.

Dawn on Sunday

Saturday night. More precisely, dawn on Sunday. I'm on my way home after spending half the night with Iim, Pon and Suket. Suket was the one driving, speeding down the roads around Kuningan. I can still feel the cold wind brushing my cheeks, still hear the roar of the car's engine in my ears. I remember how we laughed at the banci[*] clutching the lamp posts, their mouths wide open, tambourines trembling in their arms as we sped past. Iim said the shock was good for them. A reminder that in this life there's always something to laugh about and make your heart drop. And we laughed so hard. So many hilarious things happened, too many for me to recall. At the end of the night, Suket suggested we go somewhere else next week. He said there was likely to be a police raid. It's all over the news these days, the police crackdown on street racing. Now there's less about the USA and Iraq, they have to cover more local news.

Shit, I have a headache. Maybe I drank too much beer, or whatever was in those plastic bottles Pon brought. Pon is kind of a cool friend. He never forgets to bring some food and drink along, meaning the four of us are always satisfied. At least in terms of alcohol. I stop my car at the red light under the overpass. It's so quiet. Almost every Sunday, in the same spot, I see a guy sat twirling his dirty

[*]   Banci - derogatory term for waria

handkerchief. Maybe this is his patch. He always stares at me, his gaze unblinking. It makes me want to get out of my car and punch in his greasy head, but I always suppress the urge. I don't know why, but each time it makes me feel cold all over. I glance quickly over to where he usually sits. He's there, shirtless and waving the dirty handkerchief in his hands. I want to see him clearly. Staring across at him, I see his little eyes staring back at mine. He's not as young as I imagined. Maybe he's older than me. Not as tall, though. And very thin. Suddenly a chill runs through my body. I shiver, feeling cold. I regret driving this way. The red light has been on for too long, and that guy... Quick as a flash he jumps up and walks towards my car. It happens so fast. I go to push the lock button down, but it's too late. He's much quicker than I am. By the time the lights change, he's already sitting next to me. I try to shove him out of the car, but he's strong, his body overpowering mine. His hands tighten firmly around my wrists. The stench of his body odour pierces my nostrils. His body moves quickly over my shoulders.

'Drive!' he snaps at me. He stares into my eyes, ready to attack. Letting go of my wrists, he swiftly moves his right hand to my neck, while he reaches for something with his left. I feel a sharp cold object touch the skin above my heart. I look down, trying to see what it is. He cackles. 'Fork. Rusty.'

My only option is to do as he says and drive off. But where to? I don't know and don't have the courage to ask. I feel like there's a big ball stuck in my throat. From the rear-view mirror, I see there's a car behind. My head hurts.

My mouth feels so dry. I glance into the rear-view mirror again, but the car behind has gone. My head spins fast. I feel like I want to throw up.

'Just drive to your house,' he whispers. He loosens his grip slightly, though he holds the rusty fork in the same place, pressing it harder. 'It feels good. Riding in a car.' He's grinning, large teeth protruding from behind his lips. 'A good car.' His eyes dart back and forth, taking it in.

'Hmmm…' I try to answer him but all that comes out is a murmur. My voice has disappeared.

'Can you race this car? Is it fast enough?' He leans in, our foreheads almost touching. So close the beads of sweat on my brow could moisten his dark wrinkled forehead…

'Is this your car? Eh? Eh?'

I shake my head quickly.

'Stop shaking your head like that! Talk to me! What do you think I am? A robber? I'm no thief! I just want to go for a drive. I want to go for a drive in a nice car!' His voice rings through my ears.

I cough, trying to speak up. 'No… No… This is my father's car…'

'Your father's pretty rich, isn't he?' he sneers. I don't know whether I should smile, nod, or shake my head. 'I always wanted to work at the car factory. I went to school. Mechanical school. But only for three months. I didn't have the money to pay the fees.'

'Oh…' is all I say.

'It must be great, being well-educated. You've a rich father, can go to university, get bought a fancy car to drive…' I try to swallow, but my saliva tastes bitter in my mouth.

'I have six brothers and sisters, all younger. My father is a street sweeper. He used to work at the factory, but one of his fingers got cut off. So he couldn't work anymore. It's been tough on all of us.' He places the fork on the dashboard. 'It's not as easy as you think, looking for a job these days. I want to be a newspaper seller, but I need a guarantor. The only work I can get right now is washing cars, polishing the mirrors. If they're not happy with your work, they give you a quick cash payment and hurry you away. Plus, look at me... I'm shirtless! A lot of people get scared!' he laughs. I nod. 'You keep nodding away like a parrot. Are you scared I'm going to kill you?' He smiles like he can read my mind. 'Have you ever seen a man get run over by a car?' I shake my head. 'It's horrible, when he's not quite dead yet. When he's still flailing around like a rooster,' he says. 'Have you ever run over a rooster?' I shake my head again. He jerks his shoulders, as if shivering. Maybe the rush of wind blowing in through the window has made him cold. 'Do you like to race your car like those bastards?' I know what he's on about, though I decide to shake my head in answer. 'Don't do it. There have been too many victims already. My little sister died because of those stupid people. She got mown down by a car that was wild racing down the road. She was unlucky. She didn't die immediately. She flew up through the air like a rooster. Her blood was everywhere.'

I want to throw up, unable to stomach any more of his story. But this crazy guy next to me won't stop talking. I decide I don't care anymore, thrusting my head out of the window.

'Red stains everywhere. Pity. Her name was Endang. It was so unlucky… Her first day selling mineral water on the roadside and she got hit. Mak lost her mind in the space of a week, screaming and running down the street where it happened. You seem like a nice guy. I hope you grow up to be a good person. That you'll be rich…'

His voice is calm and gentle. He takes a deep breath and closes his eyes. 'Were you scared?'

I nod. I was afraid I might die. I'm a little calmer now, but the fear is still there.

He laughs. 'If you were a bad person, if it was you who'd hit my little sister, then I'd kill you. But I know it wasn't you. I can see you're terrified of everything. Chicken shit!' He laughs loudly and I can see his molars. I give a slight smile. Shit.

'What's your name?'

'Aca.' My voice sounds like it's been squeezed through two heavy iron pipes.

'Ha! That's hilarious. Like a girl's name.' He laughs loudly. He points his index finger at a tree at the side of the road. 'Pull over here, would you.' I bring the car to a stop where he says. He opens the door and jumps out quickly. 'Careful not to kill people!' he calls back, grinning. And then as speedily as he'd jumped in my car, he vanishes behind a tree, fast as lightning.

I take a deep breath. I hope this is all just a dream, brought on by my headache and the glare of the red light. But everything seems so real. I've reached the east of Jakarta already, driving all the way from where I picked him up.

I stare into the darkness, but he's disappeared. I close my window, lock the doors and drive off. I want to go home. Instinctively, I put my hand on the seat he was sitting on. It feels cold, but how can it... No matter how slight he was, his body would still have left a little warmth on the seat. I touch it again. It really is cold. I look for the fork he put on the dashboard. Nothing. Just a small dried up twig, shaped kind of like a fork. When I reach out to touch it, I find the edges are brittle, breaking off in my hands like ash. The air is chillingly cold. It wasn't a dream. It can't have been. I can still feel his grip on my neck. And the rusty fork digging into my chest. It's morning already. I've been awake all night. I've got to do something now. Call Pon, Suker and Iim. I'm going to cancel next week's meet-up. It's over. Never again.

I Am a Man

She is so beautiful. So very beautiful. I don't know why I've only just noticed the beauty of this girl. Where have I been all this time? Don't ask. I don't have an answer. Honest.

Every morning, when I arrive at college, I'm always watching for her shadow. I wait for her to pass in front of me. Crossing from one corridor to another, stepping from foot to foot like she's dancing on air. Quickly, without a sound. She moves so quickly that it's hard for me to see her face, which is always hidden behind her shoulder-length hair. Her hair, yes her hair is definitely very special. Our college building is full of open spaces, letting the wind blow in from different directions. She, yes, that beautiful woman, never worries about the wind ruffling her hair. She lets every strand of hair play freely in the wind. Blowing up here and there. She looks like she never needs to comb or tidy it. She just leaves it down. It doesn't matter: she's beautiful.

There was nothing special in our first meeting. It wasn't planned. A friend of mine introduced her to me. By mistake, when he was having lunch in the cafeteria with this beautiful woman. I showed up all of sudden, so my friend felt like he was the host in some way and then he had to introduce us. She smiled and shook my hand. Firmly. Confidently. I like this kind of handshake. Not limp, not sweaty. She didn't talk very much. But what little she did say, as my friend was telling his stories, was quite surprising. She wasn't like any of my other friends. She loved reading. She was smart. She – without making any effort at all – was clearly a genius. I asked for her phone number. She gave it to me straightaway, without asking for mine in return. She didn't ask me to give her a call someday. She didn't care. Then her watch alarm went off and she left abruptly. There was going to be a little party at her house: today was her mum's birthday. She hopped off the cafeteria seat. She ran off. And disappeared. Just like that. Without looking back to see me, wishing I could put my hand round her shoulders. Follow her as she went. Everywhere. Together.

That's ridiculous.

Two days later, I – as the result of a lot of effort – managed to bump into her again. She still remembered my name! I was screaming happily inside my heart. I said, 'It's amazing, I can't believe you remember me.' She laughed. She said, 'Who doesn't know you – you're a college student who is pretentious enough to star in a soap opera and now insists on becoming a singer too.' I could only laugh. I didn't know what to say. I laughed merrily. It was awkward, though, because it sounded quite forced. She smiled. Maybe she couldn't wait for me to finish laughing, because then she touched my hand. She said she had to go to class. Her class was going to begin in five minutes. I just nodded, like a total fool. She left.

In the evening, while I was waiting for filming to start, I sat on my own in the corner. Suddenly I remembered her forehead, which wrinkled when she was listening to me. I remembered her touching my hand. I remembered the yelp of her laugh. I remembered the colour of her hair. I remembered her clothes, which were almost all white. I remembered every single thing about her and also how stupid I was. That night, my director wasn't happy. I couldn't concentrate. I had already forgotten all of the script. It was all too much. When I arrived home, it was already the next day. My eyes were wide awake. I couldn't sleep.

It was too much.

Don't bother telling me what you think or what to do. I know what's happening right now: I'm falling in love. I, the object of desire of so many beautiful, stunning women, I can't handle my feelings for this woman. My friends say I've become so stupid recently. Sure! My director says I'm no fun anymore. Exactly! My mother says I look like a sick hen. She's right! They all say, this can't carry on for much longer, can it? But really? Oh, it's hard! So very hard!

It's been three days now since I've been at college. I had some filming out of town. I really want to see her. I really want to hold her. Kiss her lips, play with her hair. But that's impossible. At least right now. I've had a headache this whole time. I'm in a terrible mood from morning to night. Everyone in the crew keeps running away, avoiding me. My face feels so hot. My head feels ready to explode. I want to go home soon. I turn on my mobile phone, I look for her name, and try to call her. I miss her.

On the third ring, she answers. She sounds fine. While I can barely breathe. I ask her what she's doing right now. She's reading, she says. She asks me what I'm doing right now. I get nervous. I laugh in a weird way and it doesn't sound funny to anyone who hears it. She doesn't laugh with me. My throat is getting dry, my mouth tastes bitter. We're both silent. And I panic when she says that, since I don't have anything to say, maybe I should hang up. I say quickly that I've been thinking about her and I want to chat. She laughs softly. She says she's been feeling the same. I jump so high. My phone falls down, crashing into the stones. The call ends.

Stupid!

I get back the next night. First thing the next morning I'm already sat in the corridor. Waiting for her. After the second lesson, she turns up. She waves. I run over to her. I say I'm sorry about our weird conversation yesterday on the phone. She laughs. She pats my shoulder with her hand. My body feels light as cotton. Flying. So high. I don't want to come down. I ask if she'd like to eat with me in the cafeteria after her class. She agrees. But she can't stay for very long. She has a piano lesson, she says. I say okay. Then she's gone. I go back to sitting in the corridor. I can't move. I don't want to.

Let it be.

We were just drinking coffee! We didn't end up eating. She asked me about my out-of-town filming schedule. I told her with great energy. She asked me lots of things. I didn't want to stop talking. I wanted to impress her.

Sometimes she laughed out loud about the world of my soap opera. She said that even if they made her a good offer, she would rather just be a normal woman. I agreed so much. She kept an eye on her watch. 'It's getting late,' she said. I quickly offered her a lift. She thought about it for a bit and then said okay.

In the car, she flicked through my CD collection. She was pleased to find her favourite singer there. Her eyes were sparkling. She was so happy. My heart was ready to burst, because I was happy too: her favourite CD was my favourite too! I asked her about herself. She said that she'd started playing piano because her mum had encouraged her. She said she used to find it annoying because she never had any time to take a nap. But now she got a lot of joy from it. And money! She gave piano lessons to kids. She really loved the piano now. 'Me too,' I said. But I meant, 'I love you.'

Two weeks, three weeks, a month pass by. I go out with her all the time. I take her everywhere. Sometimes we have dinner. Watch movies, go to concerts, everything! One of my friends asks one day: is she my new girlfriend? I just smile. She smiles too. We haven't talked about it yet. I don't know what's going on in her head, but in my head I'm busy strategising. I have to declare my feelings. I don't care what she says in response. I have to do it soon. I can't wait any longer.

For two days I practise in front of the mirror, moving my hands, moving my head, lifting my eyebrows, making my smile wider. I practise exposing my heart. The more I practise, the more I feel I'm doing it all wrong. I don't manage to convince myself. I try to remember the script of a scene with a love declaration that I did in the soap opera. It's bad. I feel so odd. I can't believe myself. Everything I say sounds boring, or strange. I want to throw up after listening to myself. This is too much! Why, when my feelings are so strong, can't I get it right? Why? I'm finding it hard to breathe.

Oh god.

The night before I'm going to meet her, I can't sleep. I look up at the ceiling of my room. Searching for the answer that's not written there. Whether I want to or not, I have to say something tomorrow. I must! I've learned them by heart, the words I've been practising, even though I don't think they're good enough. I hope I'll get some inspiration tomorrow for making my declaration better.

And here we are. In her living room. I feel like the couch I'm on is trying to eat me up. As for her, she's in a good mood. She's busy talking about the book she's just finished reading. 'It's about a woman who wrote about her mother's life,' she says. I'm sure she doesn't know why I'm here. I force myself to smile widely. Sweat is dripping down my back. My throat feels so dry, though I keep swallowing. I want to scream. I want to groan! I want to swear. Why is it men who have to say 'I love you' first? Why must men do this? Why does the world believe that men will find this easy? Nothing simpler? Who thinks that? Who?

Suddenly my voice leaps out. I hear it coming out of my mouth. It sounds like this: 'Can I be your boyfriend?'

My hands are trembling, clutching a cushion. I am a man with a million female fans who all say they adore me – but I break into a cold sweat between my toes when telling a woman that I love her.

One second, two seconds, she's still talking about the book, whatever it's called. I can't breathe. Five seconds, then she turns her head. Stares at me as I wince. Her eyes narrow. Her lips open. My heart is beating faster. Then I hear her voice: 'What did you just say?' She didn't hear me! I want to faint right now! It's so hard being a man!

An Apology

The graduation ceremony is happening right now in Jakarta Convention Center.

My mother is there. But I'm not. I'm here.

I'm here with her.

A month ago, one night in my living room, I was tidying up my dissertation, which was full of handwritten notes from my supervisor. She was sat calmly in front of me, not saying a word. I had asked her to be silent. It makes me feel awful to ask her to be quiet, because she finds it very difficult. But what else can I do? If I let her speak, she'll break my concentration with her foghorn voice. Not to mention her very loud laugh, which could genuinely deafen me. I've missed two of my dissertation deadlines now. Thanks to the kindness of my supervisor, I've been allowed an extension. If I miss this one, there go my mother's hopes of having a son with a degree.

It's so quiet here. Between the two of us, there's just the sound of a keyboard. When I try to glance over at her, she's still sitting in the same position. Her head is bowed, her face is invisible, her hands folded on the table. 'It's awkward when it's too quiet, isn't it?' I begin. I can't stand to see her so silent. She doesn't move an inch. She stays sitting upright with her eyes fixed down on the table. 'Come on, we can talk about anything.'

She raises her face as she shakes her head. 'I don't have any news today,' she says. Her voice sounds sad, floating across the living room. Suddenly she gets up and leaves me on my own. I keep working alone until the morning comes and the sun shines through the window.

Ibu is up. On her way to the kitchen, she gives me a hug and a kiss on my forehead. I immediately know there's a cup of coffee and some toast coming my way.

I wake in the middle of the night because of the long nap I took after my supervision this afternoon. Just like yesterday, the house is so quiet. Only the light outside the house and the kitchen light are on. Ibu has been in bed for a while, but she always leaves the kitchen light on. Just in case someone gets hungry in the middle of the night, she says. And I'm starving now. I hope there'll be something in the fridge that I can eat without having to warm it up.

Before I reach the kitchen, I see her sitting in the same chair as yesterday. 'Don't just sit there in the dark.' I turn on the living room light. She's smiling. 'So what's going on?' She shrugs, flashing her white teeth. Her long hair is swept over her shoulder. 'I'm hungry. I'm going to get something to eat – do you want to join me?' I invite her and she agrees, rising up from her chair and going to the kitchen. She jumps up onto my mother's kitchen table. She sits, her tiny legs dangling, swinging. She sings softly. I don't recognise the song. Her head bobs.

'You look so much happier tonight. Come on, tell me! Why are you so happy?' She's staring at me with her big round eyes. I can't believe I just asked her to speak.

'You're not going to tell me to shut up again?' Every time she speaks, I'm always stunned. Her voice sounds like a tofu's cheesecloth. It's not rounded. Not loud. Maybe it is best described as the sound of a scratch.

'Nope, I'm ready to listen.' I look for the rest of the bread I had this morning – that's all I can eat for now.

'I'm happy. I'm falling in love,' she says, this time even more softly, nearly inaudibly.

'Wow, that's amazing! Who with?' I'm curious.

'I'm not going to tell you,' she says.

'That's cheating! You started telling me something really interesting and now you're going to stop in the middle just like that? Come on, tell me – who's the lucky boy?' I press. 'You're beautiful. I'm sure that the boy you like is handsome. Is he from around here?'

She nods.

'Who? Do I know him?'

She smiles.

'Give me a clue – what does he look like? Maybe I can guess?' My curiosity is at its peak.

She is laughing hard now, which sounds as strange as her voice. My ears feel bruised.

'Don't make a racket, it's already late!' I remind her. But she can't stop. She carries on laughing. It starts to make me nervous. 'Shut up!' I yell. My head aches because of her loud laughter. She chokes. Her laughter stops. Her eyes are getting bigger. She was surprised by my shouting. Especially so late at night.

'I love hearing you laugh. Do keep telling me your stories. But please not too loud. You must know that your voice makes my ears hurt!' I quickly take her hand, to stop her crying. 'I can't stand girls who whine, you know!'

She nods. Her hands push her hair aside. I go back to the living room and turn on the TV, while chewing the hard dry bread.

'Come here and sit down.' I invite her to watch the news. It's 1 o'clock in the morning.

I let her sit in silence. The television presenter, with a tired face, reads out the same news I heard before going to bed. I'm bored. But there's nothing else on. 'Has he kissed you?'

'Who?' she asks.

'The boy you love: does he kiss you?'

She shakes her head.

'Have you kissed your girlfriend?' she asks suddenly.

I laugh, 'I have kissed my girlfriend, and I've kissed people who aren't my girlfriend.'

She's staring at me. She's surprised and annoyed to hear me laugh.

'It's perfectly normal...'

'But do you love her? I mean the girl who's not your girlfriend but who you've kissed already?' she asks, pushing her face closer to mine.

'Nope, no need to love her. I'm keen, she's keen too, I want to, she's happy... so we just do it.' I see her creased forehead; she doesn't seem to agree.

'Come on, lighten up... Kissing is fun!' I push my lips out at her. She moves back a little bit. 'Girls love my thick lips. They kiss my lips, bite them. We play with tongues, everything. It's always fun when my lips meet a girl's lips. It feels like a strong electric current is flowing. My heart beats so fast. Sometimes I sweat. Of course, that's passion.

After a minute, heaven's gates are open!' I laugh. She stays quiet. 'Do you want me to kiss you?' I push my face close to hers. She is surprised. She moves back. I can't stop laughing. And then she gets up, leaving me alone again.

I was trying to sleep when my feet felt cold like they were covered in ice. It's her fault: she's standing there at the corner of my bed. 'Where have you been? I haven't seen you for two weeks. My dissertation is handed in now!' It's hard to tell if she's smiling or not in the darkness of my room.

'Do you want to know who my boyfriend is?' she asks. I sit up and prick up my ears.

'Who is he?'

She is leaving my room, she doesn't answer my question. I must follow her. 'Come on, tell me!' I insist.

She puts her chin on the table. She isn't smiling. Her eyes are staring at me. And then, she whispers: 'You.'

Suddenly my heartbeat is getting faster. I'm trembling in my T-shirt.

What's happening? I try to release my nerves by laughing loudly.

'Are you serious?' I ask her, amidst my laughter. I look into her eyes. It seems incredible, but she really seems to be serious.

She is staring at me and wondering. She doesn't understand why her serious declaration of love has been met with my long, loud laughter. She's quiet, not laughing with me. I choke. Silence.

'Are you serious?' My laughter has stopped now. She is

sitting right in front of me. Silence. 'Are you serious?' I ask again, once I've managed to stop coughing.

She nods. I take a deep breath.

'Do you love me?' she asks. She makes it hard for me to breathe. I don't know what to say. I love seeing her dance, her long hair, her lovely lips. But love? I don't know if I can say that love is what is between us. I can't answer her simple question. 'You don't love me,' she says in her low voice, barely audible. She is close to tears. She is ready to leave when I catch her cold hand. I ask her to sit back down. I don't think she will but then she does. I shiver. I'm so cold. I don't know. I really don't know. But aside from the question of love, I really do want to kiss her pale, colourless lips. 'I'd better leave,' she says.

'Wait!' I hold her. She's looking at me desperately. I know she doesn't know what I want. I know she can't possibly know. Because I myself don't really know what I want. But then I hug her. Why? I don't know. And then, without me thinking, my hand reaches for her lovely face and I kiss her tightly-shut, cold lips. She is trying to get me to let her go. But my hands are stronger than hers. I continue to kiss her until she stops struggling. Slowly, her cold hands reach around my neck. Her lips start to part, letting in my tongue which has been pressing on them for a while now.

And then suddenly a burst of air enters my mouth. Cold and bitter, so strong, it crashes through until it hurts my throat. Then I feel salty water between my teeth. My mouth is sore: her sharp teeth are gripping my lips. She doesn't raise her head. Her eyes are tightly closed. I try to pull back my tongue, which is starting to freeze because of the cold and bitter air flowing into my throat, flowing down to my fingers, my toes. It keeps flowing, it makes my head dizzy. Everything is spinning around, whizzing. I try once more to get free, but she holds me tight. I can't breathe. I can't get any oxygen into my nose. I really can't breathe. I can't!

Furiously I try to drag my head back from her face. I try so hard to scream. No sound comes out. I need oxygen. I feel cold, so cold. I try to take her hands off of my neck. Useless.

This afternoon, all the students graduated. They lined up neatly. My mother represented me because I wasn't there. I was here. That night, just after the kissing, I couldn't breathe anymore. Forever. I am dead, that's what I heard. The bitter air she blew into my mouth took me into her world. She asked for an apology because it wasn't what she wanted. It happened because I had wanted it, she said. I disagreed. 'I think you knew the risk,' she explained. No, I didn't know. I didn't even think about it. 'I'm sorry,' she said, holding my hands in her hands, which weren't as cold as before. 'I am sorry,' she said. She held her face close to my face. So close. Her lips were touching my forehead, eyebrows, cheeks, nose, lips… and we kissed again. And again.

In front of us, Ibu is sitting alone, holding a wet pillow, watching a black TV screen. While we kiss again.

Cik Giok

Do not forget to buy a ticket for Cik Giok for her trip to Jakarta.

Do not forget to pick Cik Giok up at the port.

Do not forget to get the dress ready for Cik Giok.

In the middle of my wedding planning meeting, I have to wonder why Dad is so keen to take care of Cik Giok's every need. Why is Cik Giok the most important person right now, even more than me, Dad's only child who is about to get married? The most unbelievable thing is, every time Dad makes his suggestions, Mum (who rarely agrees with Dad) remains passive and silent. Emak,[*] who usually supports Mum's opinions, has also lost her voice.

It's been a long time since Cik Giok lived with us. Long before I was born. According to my family tree, I have to call her A'i Giok. Dad says that Cik Giok is the adopted child of Emak, my grandma. But since everybody calls her Cik Giok, I just call her the same. No one's had a problem with this so far.

Cik Giok's parents and Emak all lived in a village in Pontianak. Dad says that Cik Giok's parents were poor. They struggled to survive, not least because they had so many children. A year after Cik Giok was born – she was the youngest of eleven brothers and sisters – her mother became very ill. To save the life of the mother and a

---

[*]   Emak - grandmother in Chinese Indonesian

daughter, they proposed that Emak should adopt Cik Giok. Emak agreed. In our house, Cik Giok stayed in the back room, near the kitchen, next to the warehouse. It's not exactly that the room was the ugliest, but it was certainly the simplest one. Really small. Half of the wall was made of bricks. The other half was made of chicken wire covered in cheap muslin that was always washed every Saturday morning.

Why Saturday, I asked Cik Giok once. She said Saturday was the best day. If she cleaned the room on Saturday, she could then enjoy her Sunday, lying in bed without being bothered by the dusty and dirty curtains. Emak forbade me from playing in Cik Giok's room. She said her room was stuffy and humid. Not ideal for a child with asthma. Unfortunately I was totally obsessed with this room, or maybe it was just that I liked spending time with her. Especially in the afternoon, when my own room felt so hot; when Cik Giok's curtains seemed to dance in the wind, like they were calling me, inviting me to feel the coolness there. When she was less busy (she always helped Mum to cook, wash clothes, iron, clean the house and take care of Emak), Cik Giok would occasionally have time to help me with my homework.

But the thing we did together most often was swap stories. I would always complain about classes at school, especially Maths, and she would tell me stories about her remote village or repeat the story about me when I was a baby. She said I was always whinng, a real crybaby, but I was always calm when Cik Giok held me. In the middle of her story, I would often become very sleepy. Then Cik

Giok would immediately offer me a soft pillow. Then she would stroke my eyebrows till I fell asleep. Then in the afternoon, before Emak woke up from her nap, Cik Giok would shoo me from her room.

I didn't realise how close I'd been with Cik Giok until she suddenly went away. I was in sixth grade. It was close to my final exams, and I remember Cik Giok had been crying a lot. Emak and Mum told me not to go into her room. When I tried to find out what was going on, Cik Giok just shook her head and stroked my hair. It's okay, she said, trying to smile. The next day, when I got home from school, I saw that her room was empty. Mum said Cik Giok' parents were ill. That night, I didn't sleep at all. Nor the night after that. I even cried on my own in her room. Emak dragged me back out again.

She asked, Why are you crying for Cik Giok? There's no point! She doesn't remember you. She's not coming back today. This made me worry even more. I was so sad. But I tried really hard to hold my tears. I didn't want to make Emak angry.

One month, three months, six months passed. An entire year passed before I buried my hopes of ever seeing Cik Giok again. Eventually I forgot there ever was a room in the corner of our house, which I'd spent so much time in. Cik Giok had been erased from our family history. Until last week, when they mentioned her repeatedly at my wedding preparation meeting. Cik Giok has to be informed and invited, she has to be dressed up very well… So I gather that Cik Giok is coming. After disappearing

14 years ago, she will step foot in this house again. She will sleep in her room again. Mum asked our household assistant to clean up her room. Will she come back and live with us again? I asked Mum.

No, she will go back to her village after your wedding party, Mum answered.

And Cik Giok really did make it – she's on her way now. Dad has picked her up from Tanjung Priok. I'm watering Mum's Japanese frangipani when Cik Giok and Dad come down from the bajaj. I run to greet her. We hug tightly. So you're getting married, Lin? she asks, rubbing my forehead. I beam like a little girl who's been caught stealing a mango from a neighbour. Her face hasn't changed too much: serious, a bit sad. Her cheeks used to be chubby; now they're sunken. Grey hair. I grab the bag from her arms. I lead her into the house. In the living room, with her creased forehead, Mum asks Cik Giok how she is.

Good. Everything's alright, we're all fine, she replies. Emak, who hasn't risen from the table, snorts loudly. Cik Giok cups her hands, offers respect to Emak, then goes on ahead of me to her old room. I follow from behind. Just like before.

Early in the morning, Cik Giok has been busy in the kitchen. She prepares breakfast for everyone: me, Dad, Mum, and Emak. Congee with tung cai, grilled and salted fish, pickled cucumber and salted egg with dark yellow yolks. All fresh from the village. We tuck in, delighted. Cik Giok watches us from the kitchen door.

Please eat with us, Cik, I say.

I've had my breakfast, she says. When Mum lifts her face from the porridge bowl, Cik Giok hurriedly vanishes. I am ready to get up, to bring her back. But then I see Emak's face and I decide to sit down. I finish my congee.

In the afternoon, I have my wedding dress fitting. I say I want to invite Cik Giok to come with me. Mum looks unhappy, but she raises her voice and calls out to Cik Giok.

Come with us, Cik, says Mum. Cik Giok looks confused. Come see Aline try on her wedding dress, explains Mum.

I see her blushing. A smile plays around the corners of her lips. But then her smile disappears when I tease her about whether she wants to try a wedding dress too. Mum pinches my arm. Ouch! That hurt! Mum is leading Cik Giok out of the house. We walk along the boulevard, looking for bajaj. We don't talk much the entire way.

My dress is almost finished. Though it's still a bit too big on the waist, this sequined white with flower embroidery is perfect already. I'm turning around and looking at myself in the mirror. Cik Giok watches but says nothing; she doesn't even smile. We stop by the kue basah* maker for the tea ceremony, then on to the printshop to order the wedding invitations. On our way home, we still have to go by the tailor for the family outfits. The dress for Cik Giok has been chosen. It's exactly the same as Mum's, but in different colours. A little darker.

Cik Giok doesn't say a word until we get home.

---

* Kue basah - traditional cakes made (mostly) from rice flour, glutinous rice flour, and tapioca flour

I haven't slept properly for three nights now. Mum says it's normal. Especially as the big day is getting closer. She also says that all future brides are just the same. Because they are really excited and happy. Maybe. My body feels tired. My eyes are getting heavier. I leave my room, looking for something to eat in the kitchen. But when I see the fridge, filled with so many foods, I suddenly feel full. I see the light on in Cik Giok's room. She is still awake. I go in without knocking. I see her writing something. She looks surprised to see me. Is everything okay? she asks.

I can't sleep, Cik, I say. She is tidying up her papers.

Don't you feel tired? she asks me.

I just shrug. Then I sit on her bed. My legs are too long to fit on her bed that always seemed so big to me when I was young.

Who are you writing to, Cik?

My family in the village. They're quite worried about me. I'm old, I can't walk very far. I have to let them know that I've arrived in Jakarta. Safe and healthy.

Oh. That is the last thing I remember her saying. I sleep. I don't know for how long. Then I am woken up by Cik Giok's voice.

Wake up, hurry! Emak is looking for you, she says. I jump up, run to the shower. Too late, Emak is already standing in the doorway. She is so angry! Emak doesn't say a word to me until the evening. Mum is the same, only frowning sourly. In the evening, Kuku, Dad's big sister comes. In the living room, we discuss the tea ceremony we'll have with my future husband's family, twelve days from now.

I'm not sure where she comes from, but suddenly Cik Giok is standing in the kitchen doorway. She's holding a plastic chair in her hands. Her face looks so strained. Kuku asks her to come in. But her invitation disturbs Mum and Emak. In a loud voice, Mum tells Cik Giok not to sit with us. Emak is crying. Dad just disappears, although earlier he was sat calmly next to Emak. I run to Cik Giok's room. Empty. By the time I get back to the living room, Cik Giok is gone. Mum is busy trying to calm down Emak, who is crying louder and louder. I am ready to go after Cik Giok, but Kuku takes my hand. You'd better take care of Mum, she says.

What's wrong? I ask.

She tells me that someday I'll understand what's going on. Everything will be clear someday. Whenever that is. She also hugs the crying Emak.

I'm left with all my questions. What's wrong with them? What's wrong with my wedding? What's wrong with Cik Giok? With a dizzy head and messy heart, I go back to my room. I lock my door from the inside.

Tomorrow morning, I wake too late. Cik Giok has already gone. Mum says she has some urgent business in Bandung. She will be back before the wedding party. Whatever Mum says, I'm quite sure that Cik Giok won't be coming back to our house. Not even for my wedding.

A month after my extravagant wedding party, Mum asks me to come home. It's important, she says.

When I get home, Emak, Dad, Mum and Kuku are waiting in the kitchen. You have to go to Pontianak with

Dad, says Mum. Cik Giok has had a stroke.

I don't want to go. But my husband encourages me. He says that this might be the last time I'll see her.

Two days later, Dad and I travel to Pontianak. Cik Giok is already in the ICU. My stomach is churning.

Cik Giok didn't wait for me. She died one hour before we landed. Her sister, who has a similar face to her, greets us. She hugs me tight. Her tears have drenched my hair. Dad stays silent, turns away, wipes his tears.

In the funeral home, all the crying women are already beating their bodies, ringing small bells. Cik Giok looks so beautiful in her cheong sam. I cry. Dad cries louder than me. His hand tries to hold Cik Giok's stiff body. I'm sorry, he says again and again. Everyone is crying, howling while trying to get close to me, hold me. So tight, till I can barely breathe. Cik Giok's sister kisses my cheeks with her wet face.

Pay your respects to your Mama, she whispers.

Our World

I can see my reflection in the mirror. My hair seems to be growing longer. I'm quite happy with that. If I can just hang on for another month, the back of my hair will blow out beautifully in the wind. I'll look so sharp. Just be patient. Yes, I can be patient. It's no big deal, waiting for a month. It'll be worth it for the looks of admiration – or jealousy – from the students at junior high later on. That will be so awesome. But… if Ibu sees it. Yeah, my mother. Gah, this is such a nightmare! Will she be able to handle my hairstyle?

Sometimes Ibu confuses me so much. She never lets my hair grow longer than an army cadet's. If my hair covers my ears a little bit, she panics. And that's just for one or two minutes – she can't bear even two hours passing by for my hair to grow even longer! And what really annoys me is when my older sister hears her nagging. She always takes my mother's side and joins in too. When that happens, it's like putting petrol on the fire. It burns right up, noisily.

To be honest, sometimes I wonder deep in my heart, has Ibu ever looked around on her way to work or back again? Has she seen the hairstyles of kids my age? Maybe not. Maybe she's more interested in the sales or discounts offered by boutiques or malls for clothes or groceries. Or she's too busy thinking about her work, so much that sometimes she brings some of it home. Her job must be pretty important if all the tasks have filled her mind to the extent that she hasn't noticed that the *Top Gun* haircut is so yesterday. Even Tom Cruise, Ibu's idol, has changed his hairstyle now.

This is the era of Linkin Park. But also Van Morrison is in again. Sure, there's Eminem, but Foo Fighters are so much cooler. I explain this to Ibu (over and over again) but she just pats my head, like when I'm in elementary school. Maybe I'm not convincing enough? Or I should explain it more loudly. I can't stand it!

I'm worried that Ibu has forgotten I'm not in junior high anymore. I'm a high school student, even though it's only been a few months. These school years will be the most glorious time in my life, my late Bapak told me a long time ago. So I should enjoy them, right? This is what Jodi's (my classmate who sits behind me) brother said to me too. He said this is the perfect time for getting crazy and having lots of fun without feeling guilty. I agree!

My sister says high school is the time to learn how to be an adult (which means learning to be more responsible). But whatever she says, I've been waiting for this since I was in junior high. To be honest, back then I'd always be jealous when I saw the boys in grey trousers that covered their knees completely. All the way through junior high, I'd get so annoyed by girls staring at the curly hair on my legs. It made me furious when they stared and then giggled. Unfortunately, it didn't just happen once. It was many times. All the time.

Since my name was put on the list for my favourite high school, I've been so ready to begin my new life. I will be someone else. Someone new. I'm ready to forget Naruto. I'm no longer a fan of American Idol. My life now is all about Metallica, Maroon 5, adult magazines with Kelly Brook on the cover (I buy them every time I see her; I would just subscribe if I got more pocket money). I'm mature now. I'm a high school student. Remember that. Look at my room: it's covered with posters of my idols. Every time I open my door after taking a shower, their faces welcome me with their warmth. Then there's the loud music booming fiercely through my ears. This is awesome! Whoooa!

'Hey, why are you screaming like that?' The knocking surprises me. Ibu. It must be her. She's not gone to work today.

'I have a headache,' she says. Hmmm, she was curious, she was afraid something bad had happened to me. Ah, she didn't know I was singing along with Jim Morrison, 'Come on baby light my fiiiiiiiireeee!' This isn't good. Because usually when she starts to get curious, she comes into my room and stares at me, her body leaning back: surprised or at least 'surprised' to hear the thump of music that is too loud according to her (but perfect, in my opinion).

'My goodness, what kind of music is this? Do you know what time it is? Instead of getting ready, you'd rather listen to this crazy music. You'll be late!' she says as she walks in. 'Oh my, your hair!' Well, that's what I knew would happen: she walks in and sees strands of hair growing a few millimetres beyond my collar, she immediately launches into her long speech about neatness, about cleanliness, propriety, inappropriate matters, she'll ask questions... Damn! Her fingers touch the strands on my head, moving down to the nape of my neck. Aargh!

'What style do you call this? So messy! We'd better cut it off! I've never seen a student with hair like this. You're a new student. Don't go looking for trouble. You know sometimes there are spot-checks on students who don't comply with the school regulations, right? You'll regret it after the principal shaves you bald.'

Do you hear that? Do you hear that? Ibu always invokes the school principal when it's about a haircut. I'm completely certain that he's much too busy to inspect students' haircuts one by one. That's not his priority, Bu!

'Le,* I was young once. Your late father too. We knew exactly what was à la mode. But there's a good way and a bad way to follow trends. For high school students, it's best to have a short haircut. It's clean, it looks good, not scruffy. Not shaggy like this. This looks a mess. Your fringe has covered up your eyes. The back of your hair has started to tuck into your shirt collar. I wonder... Why are youths so weird these days.'

Now, just look at her words. She's using the language of their youth to build an argument. Of course they can never be the same, the past and the future. What was in fashion back then? The Beatles? The Rolling Stones (their hair wasn't so long). Bapak's pictures show that, when he was younger, his best look was styled using sticky hair cream, which made his hair so shiny it was blinding when

---

* Le - the shortened form of Tole, meaning young boy or son in Javanese

146

the sun shone on it. If he was outside for a long time and played in the heat, the oil melted onto his forehead. My goodness.

'What are you waiting for? Since your sister isn't working today, and you're going to school later on, you'd better go to the hairdresser right now!'

Oh no, Ibu! If I do that, my image as a cool high school student will be completely ruined. But I swallow all the words I want to say to Ibu before I can express them. It's impossible to say them out loud. She'll just slap me. So what can I do instead? I just bow and nod my head many times while looking for a reason to ask Ibu to leave my room.

Then I find a solution: I touch the towel around my waist so Ibu can see I need to get dressed. And it works. Before closing the door, she still has time to scan my wall with her sharp eyes. Her eyes get so wide as she looks at the posters of Kelly Brook and Carmen Electra. Taking a deep breath, she steps out of my room. She shakes her head repeatedly. Her forehead is very creased.

After getting dressed and brushing my hair (and randomly messing it up – just like how all my friends do with their hair, all the girls too), I grab my bag and jump out the window in my room. I am going without saying goodbye. Not because I'm angry and upset with Ibu's speech, but to avoid the threat of hair clippers. Maybe I should speak more often about the young trends to Ibu. Maybe I can borrow some foreign music magazines from Jodi, which are full of photos of rockstars. Or I should ask Amri to spend some time at my house, so Ibu can see how his hair moves when he walks so fast.

At school, just as I thought, all my friends have gathered together. Sitting down in the schoolyard, in front of the fence. They haven't gone inside the classroom yet because the previous class hasn't finished. But even if the room were already empty, we wouldn't be hurrying to go inside. We aren't that excited about our lessons.

Jodi pokes my shoulder a little bit harder and then he raises his hand: 'Give me five!' Then we laugh together. Nothing is funny, but it seems like we have to laugh. Laughing so hard and so long without saying any words. It's weird, huh? Yeah, kind of. I felt so weird in the beginning. But after I spent a month or two months in high school, I got familiar with this kind of communication – no words needed. Just put my hand in the air and slap my friend's palm, and follow that up with a long loud laugh. That's the way we greet each other. It's our code of togetherness. What's the meaning? Not important.

The schoolyard is getting crowded now, because the girls are arriving. They make so much noise. Giggling for no reason. Our eyes are on the senior students. They never see us – they think we're still kids. Not cool enough to be seen. So annoying!

Dirun – definitely not the name his parents gave him – is quiet today. His body is pressed against the pole. Usually, his voice will blare everywhere. His voice can be heard from the toilets, even if he is in the basketball court. From his expression, I know we won't be hearing his loud voice today. His face is knotted. His eyes are teary red. His hands are fists. What's wrong? I really want to ask him what's going on, since I'll sit next to him in class.

Then I'll know how to act and how to speak with him later on. But it's tricky because every time I look into his eyes, it's like he's avoiding me. What's wrong, buddy? Is your mum acting the same as mine about the haircut? Or is it about our choice to wear baggy shirts, three sizes too big for us?

Dirun always tells me all of his stories. This makes me feel proud. Just like Jodi, Dirun is actually not a new student in our school. He is repeating the year. Last year, rumour says, when it was graduation time, they couldn't find their report cards. They'd gone, they were nowhere to be seen. When they were found at last, it was already too late: all of their friends had already moved up to the next year. So that's why they stayed in the same class this year. Someone said that Dirun is so lazy, he often skips class. But when I asked him, he said it was just because of a judgemental teacher. What is the truth? Who knows? Who cares?

Dirun has so many friends in the year above, and even in the year above that, also from the morning classes. For them, Dirun isn't a kid in the year below. Dirun is their leader. If he wants, he can bring in his car (which Jodi says was modified by his mechanic neighbour who has his own garage) to take the basketball team to practise at a court near the army barracks. Or, when he has some money from threatening someone with a weapon, Dirun will buy packs of cigarettes and give them to his friends for free.

Now, imagine: the leader of the class has decided to be my friend and also he sits next to me. And that's not all: recently he has started confiding in me, telling me lots of stories every day. I'm so proud of this! Yes! Genuinely, this makes me really happy. Even more when he asks to copy my homework. Especially Physics. I don't mind this. Everybody does it. Call it a mark of my gratitude towards him.

The ringing bell signals the end of the morning class, the end of our fun chatting with friends. After that, we will be busy ourselves. Though we have time to watch the students from the classes before us. I think the girls from the morning classes are more beautiful. They're so cute and don't make too much noise. They're much better than the girls in my class!

'Mung, what's wrong with Dirun?' Jodi suddenly stands up next to me.

'Why are you asking?' I try to find Dirun. 'Where is he?'

'He's there. Having a serious conversation with a student from the morning class. See his face. So vicious. Let's catch up with him – maybe he needs help.' Jodi is waving me over.

'You can go by yourself. I don't know that guy from the morning class. Does he really need help? Maybe he's just chatting with him.'

'Are you afraid?' he asks, elbowing me.

'Afraid? Man, what, you think I'm afraid?'

'Yes, you. You're afraid of meeting Dirun and his friends. You're afraid to get in a fight. You've never been in a fight before, have you?'

'Afraid or not, it's no big deal. If he asks me for help, I'll help. But if he's fine, why should I get involved? If he gets mad, that will only complicate things!'

Jodi wants to reply, but I'm already heading to class and I don't feel like discussing this further. I'm surprised that Jodi has this weird perception of me. If my sister heard what he said, she would laugh so hard and give Jodi the new nickname 'Minister of Everyone Else's Business'.

When the bell for class rings, I see that the chair on my left is empty. Where is Dirun? I turn around to my right. Jodi isn't there either. I'm afraid that he really is in trouble. I'm so stupid – why didn't I go and help him? So stupid. All through the lesson, I don't know what's going on and what the Biology teacher is saying to us. My ears can't take anything in. My head is dizzy thinking about Dirun. I'm afraid that he is being beaten up and Jodi couldn't help him either.

In the third lesson today, we have Mathematics. The teacher, Pak Yusuf, is nowhere to be seen. Instead, Dirun appears beside me and pulls my arm. 'Come on, come with me, I'll need many guys. We're going to war!' he says. His eyes are murky, full of anger. Thank god! I have the chance to help my best friend! No need to say it twice – I'm already out of the class. In the corner of Warung Pak Baik, all my friends from the other classes are getting together. They look as furious as Dirun. Jodi is there too. He is laughing hard as usual and gives me the famous high five.

'What's wrong, Jodi? Who's attacking us?' I try to ask.

Jodi raises his eyebrows. 'No one.'

I don't understand.

'We'll be attacking first. Any problem with that?' he

says. And then he opens his bag and asks me to look at what's inside. It's a hunting dagger, just like Wesley Snipes has, but this one is cheap and fake. He is grinning. He rummages around for something else, then reaches for my hand. He gives me two small pills. I don't know what they are.

'Eat them. You'll be healthier,' he says, and then his laughter starts again. Laughing so long. So hard. He stays beside me and watches me closely. Yes, he is waiting for me to swallow the pills.

'Water?' I'm suddenly not feeling so good. What kind of medicine is in those pills? What will happen after I swallow them?

Jodi is grumbling. He says I'm like a baby, taking pills with water. But he goes and looks for water for me. He hands me a glass. My heart is beating so fast. Suddenly a horrible feeling comes over me. I can't breathe. Jodi is still waiting. He stares me down with his eyes as a command for me to swallow the pills. Medicine. What can I do? I put them in my mouth, then gulp down lots of water. Jodi isn't satisfied yet. He grabs my face and squeezes my cheeks so my mouth opens. When he doesn't find the pills in my mouth, he starts to laugh again. And hugs me tight, his eyes shining proudly. From this I can guess what he wants to say: 'Welcome to our group!' But my heartbeat is getting faster. My stomach is throbbing as well. I hope he won't ask me to open my mouth again, because they're still inside. I can't hide them much longer. When I get the chance, I have to throw them out. Far away. Without Jodi knowing.

'We're going to SMA 20 high school. Today they will get an extra sports lesson from us,' says Dirun.

'Why, Dirun?' asks one guy. I think he is in the first year, class number three.

'No reason. I just want something to do. Why? Do you have a problem with that?' he asks fiercely. That guy shuts his mouth. He raises his hands and laughs. An apology to the leader. Dirun smiles. Apology accepted. It's over.

Jodi grabs me. 'Stop daydreaming! We're going soon. Give your bag to Mr Good – that's what we call Pak Baik,' he says. I obey.

Pak Baik* shoves my bag inside an empty cardboard box and pushes it behind his bale-bale bench. Pak Baik smiles when I keep looking back at where he's put my bag. 'It's safe here. Where are you going?'

'We're going to help Dirun...' I answer him quickly, after spitting out the pills. Pak Baik looks at me. His eyebrows meet in the middle of his forehead; his grey eyes hold many questions and are looking for the answers. 'It's a kind of vitamin, Pak. But it tastes bad. It's okay to throw them away, right?' He nods. But I know he doesn't believe me, because I see many questions in his eyes.

'This seems like a general attack...' he says to me. 'I can't understand the new generation. They're just thinking about ego. They're fighting each other again and again. Aren't they tired? I'm terrified about the future of the country,' he mutters.

Suddenly Jodi is next to me, 'Mr Good, Mr Good...

---

*   Baik - good

Your children want to teach the arrogant people a lesson. Don't ask so many questions, don't give us your moralising. We don't need it. Give us support, give us ammunition and provisions. That's what we need!' he says. My heart is jumping into my throat. I really hope he didn't see what I did with the pills. He didn't. He grabs a pack of cigarettes from Pak Baik's shop. Pak Baik tries to stop him, but Jodi's hand is faster. Jodi laughs. 'Don't be so stingy with your sons, Mr Good! It's not good!'

Jodi is showing his spoils to Dirun. 'Give it to me!' Dirun yells. Jodi laughs again.

From behind, I feel someone pulling my shirt. A boy from the first grade, class 3.

'Do you still have them?' he asks me.

'How?'

'The things Jodi gave you.' Oh, he's asking for pills. I shake my head. He doesn't believe me.

'Eh, don't act so stupid! Those pills are for everyone! No favouritism here!' He speaks so loud all of a sudden. His hand grips the neck of my shirt. His breath smells of alcohol. This early in the morning? I feel like everyone is watching us. No more talking. Someone is getting closer to us. I look at... Dirun.

'Heya, idiot! What do you want?' he asks the guy. He pushes the boy from I-3 away. 'Go and sort yourself out.'

Jodi makes the sign for everyone to gather round. Just like an army of ants finding the dead body of a greenfly. All the faces are the same: furious. Vicious. The smoke from the cigarettes makes us feel like we're wrapped in fog.

Dirun draws the map he copied from a friend's book: SMA 20's map. He decides the points for attack. It feels so surreal. We're just like the Gauls, listening to a speech from Asterix, the small cartoon hero. I keep this thought to myself. I know if I laugh now, I'll be finished.

I try to concentrate on Dirun's instructions, but my friends' faces are more interesting. A deafening scream, as a symbol of agreement, stops my busy mind. We all stand in a circle. We knock shoulders, one to another, giving each other high fives. This time we're not laughing. We are so ready for war. Furious faces. But sombre.

'Any more cigarettes?' Ah the I-3 guy is approaching me. Crap! He's spotted the cigarette Dirun gave me in my shirt pocket.

'Why?' I ask him.

'You don't smoke, do you?' he grins.

'Who said that?' I answer. He's right. I'm not a regular smoker. First of all, I'm afraid of being caught by Ibu and my sister. Second of all, I don't enjoy it. But in this kind of situation, I'd better keep talking.

'Don't be ridiculous. If you want another cigarette, ask Jodi. If you're afraid, just ask Pak Baik,' I add. The I-3 guy is looking deeply into my eyes. He seems so curious about me. But luckily he doesn't have time to do anything else, as Dirun has called and we walk away.

The first part of the plan is complete: catching a mikrolet. The mikrolet* driver is watching us in the rear-view mirror. His face looks wry. He doesn't say anything. We

---

*   Mikrolet – a kind of minibus

fill his vehicle. I'm sure Dirun doesn't even think to pay the driver. Meanwhile, Jodi has stopped another mikrolet. Some boys are following him. We don't talk so much. We are looking around us. In the front seats, there is already a group of students in white-and-grey uniform. The mikrolet driver looks surprised when Dirun (who is sitting behind him) taps his shoulder hard. He immediately steps on the brakes. We jolt forward. The I-3 guy is almost thrown out of the vehicle. Dirun is upset by that. He grabs the driver's shirt; the driver's eyes are bulging, ready to escape from their sockets. 'Do you wanna die? I have a clurit* with me...' says our leader. I believe it in the deepest pit of my heart. I know Dirun is not lying about that.

'What are you doing? Come on, get out!' Dirun yells, his hands still grabbing the driver's shirt. When we are all out, he lets go. He yells for the last time at the driver, whose sweat-soaked head thuds back against the seat. Outside, Jodi, Yusuf and Inu are at the front. They are holding stones and knives and swinging their arms wildly. Next to me the I-3 guy is walking and jumping. He is yelling an endless stream of jumbled words. Suddenly I hear Dirun's voice. 'There... There...! Get them!' he screams in the midst of a group of 50 students. Together we attack the students who have just got out of school. We kick down the girls who were standing near the power pole. They're screaming so loud, like knives stabbing our ears.

The inevitable battle. Our group is quite strong. Our opponents are stunned. But before long they become as violent as us. Their hands hold the weapons. I'm possi-

---

*   Clurit - a sickle

bly the only guy without a weapon, so I try to punch in all directions. I see the I-3 guy doing well. He takes the monkey wrench (where did he find that?) and gets ready to hit someone. I can't imagine burying it in someone's head. They would be dead in an instant, that's for sure.

Suddenly, in front of me, an opponent – fortunately one without a folding knife or monkey wrench – is gripping my shoulder. Maybe he wants to break it. I hit him repeatedly. Ugh, my mouth feels salty and fishy. I touch my lips… Blood! My opponent also groans in pain. But that doesn't mean he will stop. Instead, he is showering me with punches with even more fervour than before. I try to dodge, but I lose my footing. The angry guy's fist stops at my chin. And I land firmly on the asphalt. My head spins on its axis. So dizzy. It looks like my attacker has two, four… five… faces. I shake my head. Everything goes dark.

I was unconscious. I don't remember a thing. When I open my eyes, my face and my chest are wet. Soaked. Who dared to make me all wet? I try to get up, but my stomach hurts so much. 'Hey, wake up! Wake up! Quiet! You were lucky you didn't die! Come on! Wake up!' The voice of an adult man, yelling at me, hurting my ears. A policeman! He kicks me lightly on my shoulder. When he sees me grimace in pain, he smiles. He looks so happy. That makes me unhappy. 'Now you know how it feels! You want to die? Tired of life? Idiot! There, wake up! Get in the colt!' Colt, what's a colt?* I try to follow where his finger is pointing. Wow, there are many friends and enemies sit-

---

* Colt - a Mitsubishi minivan with two benches in the back, often used by the police

ting together in the back of the van. I know where we're going: the police station.

The policeman who woke me up has zero patience for me working all this out. He can't wait even two more minutes, so he grabs my arm and pushes me towards the car. The other police officers help me get inside. Argh, my stomach feels like it has exploded. So sore. I'm sitting on the floor of the car. There's no space on the bench. All the colts drive off. I see Dirun in the first colt and Jodi in the second one, following behind. While I'm looking around, an ambulance passes by with its siren roaring.

'One of your friends is dead because of your ridiculous battle. Crazy kids!' grumbles a police officer. The hair on my neck stands on end. I'm freezing.

Finally we arrive at the police station. We are herded into the main room. On the floor, we sit topless in a row. They call us up one by one and note down our names, addresses, ages, parents' phone numbers… everything. And then we are herded into a detention room. The police officers ask us to move along, to fill the cell.

It immediately feels so cramped and stuffy inside. Too many people. We're packed together tightly. I have a headache. I want to close my eyes, but I can't. I can see Dirun sitting in the corner of the room. Deflated. And I don't know where Jodi is. But the I-3 guy, where is he? I haven't seen him since he had the monkey wrench in the battle. Next to me is one of our opponents. He grins, then grimaces in pain. He leans towards me then whispers: 'You guys, you pathetic bunch of girls, you lost a friend in the battle.' Who could it be? I shudder.

Despite being all crammed in, we manage to sleep in this tiny space. We wake up when the police officer rattles the cell door. He tells us to come out and leads us to the main room. We sit back down on the floor. We are silent. Wait. Then the police commander with his thick moustache appears. He starts talking. His voice is so loud, but I can't catch most of his sentences. My head is still dizzy.

'You... as the next generation of our country... Why did you do that... It's better when... So is that...' It's not clear enough for me. But I can guess the gist: we must never fight like this again. Every time he asks 'Understood?' we all reply 'Understood, sir!'

The small main hall is suddenly very noisy. It's because the police commander has finished his speech. We have to come forward, one by one, and sign a pledge: never to repeat our ridiculous actions ever again. Dirun smiles, and from the way his lips curve I am quite certain he won't stop getting involved with battles. Nor Jodi. I try to look at our opponents. But it's hard because we all really just want this to be over. So we don't stop to shove each other on our way to the big table. Where a big police officer is asking for our names and schools. And then hands out a letter and a pen.

'Stick this right in your heads, boys: if anything like this ever happens again, you'll go straight to prison. This is not just a warning!' Then we are finally set free. We go back to the other room and put our uniforms back on, covered with blood and soil, wet and smelly. I button up my shirt as I walk outside. The sky is dark already. In front of the office, some parents are waiting for their children.

Ibu is there. Her eyes are so red and swollen. My sister is standing beside her. She looks furious. Her face makes me afraid.

I understand why Ibu cried so much. I understand why my sister is so mad. I get it. I do. They must be disappointed in my decision. I shouldn't have joined in with this bad behaviour. I should have been strong enough not to go.

A while ago – about three months ago when I was still in junior high, I didn't have many friends. I was the quiet one. Never got into any trouble. Never smoked. Never bothered with the 'Oooooh ooooooh' pictures. I just liked playing on my friend's PlayStation. More than that, I wanted to spend time with Ibu after work, laughing together, listening to stories about her boss. Or teasing my sister about spending all her time with her boyfriend. When Sunday morning came around, we would get ready to cook together.

And now? So many things have changed. I wanted them. I wanted to change myself. Become the adult me. The fierce me. But I didn't know how quickly it would happen.

Ibu grabs my arm. My sister is hailing a bajaj. We head home. We don't speak to each other on the way. When we get home, Ibu goes to her room and locks the door from the inside. My sister too. I am in the living room, alone. Without making a noise, I go to the bathroom. Clean myself. And then go to my room as well. I want to sleep but I can't. My eyes stay open till the sun rises.

I'm ready for school even before Ibu and my sister wake up (this has never happened before). Without having any breakfast, I head out to school. The morning schedule begins with the flag ceremony. As I expected, we are the number one topic of the day. The students are noisy as bees flying in the air when Pak Yunus, our principal, offers his deep condolences for the death of Tino – this was the real name of the I-3 guy. He was hit and stabbed so many times. And then, silence: we are all praying for Tino. My head is spinning. My throat chokes. The ceremony is over. The other punishment awaits: we have to clean the school yard for a whole week. So annoying. Especially if our friends bother us. They deliberately drop litter where we've only just cleaned. I really want to beat them all up, but that would bring a new kind of trouble. We have to be grateful for what we've been given. Try hard to be patient.

After school, I see Ibu and my sister just act normally. They still haven't asked about what I did. Ibu doesn't seem interested in the horrific, terrible things I've done: I was in the police cell for hours. This is exactly what I'd hoped for at home: not to be judged. I don't like being scolded, mocked, blamed. I know I was wrong. But it's done now. End of story. Please don't try and pile on more guilt. But really, today, I do want to be asked about that awful day. And if it means they will grumble all day long after hearing my story, I can accept that. It would be much better than how things are now. I feel like a stranger in my home.

I want to scream at the top of my voice, so that everyone knows: I will never ever behave so stupidly again! I'll never join a battle again. It's fine to be a nerd and an outcast. I'm fine with just a few friends. I'm ready to cut my hair. Do you want me to have Clark Gable's style, Ibu? Or the young cadet's? I'll do it, Bu! And if my friends mock me? I don't give a damn. I just want us to be the same as before.

Those posters which annoy you when you come into my room? I'll tear them into little pieces. Those grungy songs that give you a migraine, Ibu? I'll give all the CDs away. The most important thing is that I'll never again cause any trouble in your life, or worry my sister, or disappoint our beloved late Bapak. Suddenly, I remember what Bapak said to Ibu: 'Honey, your protector is already here. If I'm not here, he will be your defender, he will look after you just as I have done.' A protector? A defender? How can I be those things if I can't even take care of myself? If Bapak could see me right now, I don't know if he could be more disappointed.

My period of punishment ended two days ago. Everything has gone back to normal. Wait. No. Not exactly normal. The girls in our school now avoid us every time we're near. Or if we try to get closer to them, they move away again. Maybe they're afraid of us? Or... maybe they just hate us. It's okay, we deserve their hate. We're the ones who let our friend get killed, right?

Our places in class have been totally changed and switched around by our homeroom teacher. We, the former offenders, are in the front row of the classroom. Di-run is no longer next to me. He sits right in front of the teacher's desk. Jodi is on the right. I am on the left. To be honest, I'm quite happy with these changes. At least we won't be whispering during the lessons anymore, or handing each other ridiculous notes.

When it's break time, in a minute, I go straight to the basketball court. The bell rang a few minutes ago. But Pak Suyadi and his biology lesson haven't come out yet. The classroom is the same: so noisy. Everyone's mouths chatting unstoppably. Everyone wants to talk to each other. Everyone wants to get out of the class. Suddenly someone is pulling on my shirt. Jodi! We haven't talked much since we were moved. I don't want to. His crooked teeth showing in an annoying grin. Without saying a word, he points out the window: Dirun! That kid wasn't here this morning.

'There's another job waiting for us,' whispers Jodi.

I have goosebumps. I look at him and, with all the force I have, I make myself say: 'Sorry, you'll have to go by yourself, man.'

Jodi stares at me. He can't believe it. He shakes his head. His smile twists. He looks disgusted at the sight of me. Then he does the thumbs-down. This is a code for Dirun. The guy with acne on his face rushes into the classroom. His right hand shoves Jodi and the other grabs me by the shirt neck. I feel cold sweat dripping down my back.

'So you want to be a good guy now, eh? Do you want to die too?' His right hand is free now, feeling around for something. Behind his thin shirt I can see something I often see in action movies. A gun! 'Dirun… Please, don't!' I don't remember saying anything else. My tongue feels stiff. My eyes feel hot. Suddenly I can see what happened to that I-3 boy: his body was trampled by the enemies, his hands tried to stop them but it was useless, while red flowed from his mouth… It feels so real, so imminent.

It's so clear. I shake my head. The vision fades. Dirun is gripping my neck and moving my head up and down. I am nodding to his request. In a flash, I get up on the table, leap out of the window. I am out of the class. Jodi follows behind. Three of us are running out the fence. There, many friends are waiting. Ready for a new battle. For the second time, I am not ready. I am unarmed. But still I am going. Joining the battle.

In this next battle, we lose another friend and injure a police officer (his head cracks, hit by a brick). In one week, the newspapers can't stop reporting on this. Everyone feels like it's important to have an opinion about it. The psychologists and social experts offer many different theories. This no longer feels like the soul-refreshing experience like Jodi said it was. We stay in the prison cell for two days. But this time there are even more of us. Unbearably cramped. Every morning we are woken up by cold water tossed over us from buckets.

Ibu comes back to pick me up. My sister too. Just like before, we remain silent on the way home, but I really want to tell her about the tiny prison cell with so many people inside. About the strong light which is always on, hurting my eyes, but which can also make you sleepy. About the loud sound of the radio. About the officers' voices. Sometimes they laughed amongst themselves. Not to mention the arguments between us: the attackers and the defenders. I want to tell her about these experiences. But Ibu and my sister just stare straight ahead. Silent. Why don't they go on and on like before? If that's what they want to do, I know I'll feel better. But now I just suffer inside. I want Ibu to hug me. I want my sister to poke my shoulder, ruffling my hair in the way that shows she loves me. I want to ask them to do all that but instead I just have to look down at the trembling bajaj floor.

The early morning prayers filter in through my ears. The fresh air makes me feel sleepy and want to stay in bed. But not right now, not today. I have to wake up early. I've got lots of things to do. It's almost a month since I moved out of Ibu's house. I decided I needed to flee. I thought it best to go and stay with Mbah (my grandmother) in the village, where she's been on her own for a long time. Before I arrived, Mbah was surrounded with chickens, a goat, and a pair of ducks that were busy running around in her little yard. Occasionally – twice a week – a neighbour's child would come and help her out, cleaning the yard and bringing over food. Now I do all those things. Ibu cried a lot when I decided to leave. My sister didn't want to talk to me. They thought it was a silly decision.

'Do you need to go far away to be a better person?' Ibu said, just after I told her about my plan. 'Ibu and your sister will help you. It's not easy being a high school student now. A good child can be mean if he has mean friends. I understand, Le. Ibu will help you. Your sister too. The important thing is you have to tell us about everything. Tell us your story! We used to discuss everything. You told me everything about your friends, your school – everything. But now you keep yourself hidden.'

I understand what she meant. And I trust her love for me, for everything she does to keep me on the right track. Who would doubt the abilities of Ibu? The problem lies with me. I've caused so much trouble for Ibu. I am a troublemaker. I should be making her happy and calm. I should be making her proud about me. I'm the only son she has, I should have been her protector. Taking good care of her. But what happened? Ibu was the protector 24 hours a day for a big kid like me. And there's no guarantee that I wouldn't get into any trouble again. It was tough at school, I started the year with the wrong crowd – the wrong friends. I didn't have the courage to reject danger-ous behaviour. When they gripped my neck, I would go along with whatever they wanted. Such a chickenshit. I was so ashamed of myself.

I love Ibu. I love my sister too. That's why I'd do any-thing to make them happy. I don't want to add to Ibu's burden. Same for my sister. I know my decision made her sad. But I believe this might be the better way for all of us: Ibu, my sister and me. If my plan works, we can live our lives in peace. Only one thing will sadden us: we won't be under the same roof. We can call each other an-ytime, though. The distance from Jakarta to Ngasem can be crossed by bus or train.

So yes, I ran away to the village: that's what the ru-mours said about me at school, that's what my friends wanted to hear. I don't care. The important thing is that I don't have to run every time they ask me to run. I have a new school here. A school between the rice fields, far away from the big streets. My teachers come to school by bicycle, motorcycle or andong.* We, the students, go on

*   Andong - a horse-drawn carriage

foot. Some students ride bicycles, but not so many. Sometimes I think about my friends in my old school. How would they react if they could see me now? They would surely pile on: look at this countryside boy! But I really don't care what they think. I'm safe here. I'm no longer being chased. Who cares about the new trends, new metal bands, new hairstyles…

I have a new hairstyle now: just like a young cadet. The kind of music I listen to now is macapat.* Or keroncong. Mbah isn't too familiar with campur sari, much less English songs! Macapat and keroncong used to make me feel lonely. However, after twenty days, everything is getting better. I enjoy everything that comes to my ears, I enjoy every taste on my tongue. Maybe I'm a real countryside boy now. Who cares? I'm happy here. There is just one more important thing in the world than that: I'm preparing myself to be a real protector for Ibu. Just like Bapak said before.

Someone knocks at my door. Mbah has already woken up. I've spent so much time in my room now. It's time to start my daily task. 'Yes, Mbah… I'm already up…' I reply. Outside the sun is already shining, the sky already bright. The smell of wet grass wafts into my nose.

What a beautiful day it will be.

---

*   Macapat - a traditional recited Javanese poem in a song form, accompanied by gamelan

167

One Fine Morning

Mornings are the worst for me. It's because, early every morning, I'm forced to wake up immediately – not by the sunlight, but by all the fuss at home: the whooping of the kids and the yelling of their mother. Not to mention the constant slamming of doors.

I always ask them, very diplomatically, to make less noise, be less frenzied early in the morning. But the mob – by which I mean my daughter, son-in-law, the grandchildren, the babysitter, our household assistant – just keep behaving exactly the same. Every day. Every morning. It's getting worse and worse. I've tried to ask them in different ways, from gentle, grumpy, quiet, weeping... It makes no difference! If they do ever take it on board, it only lasts for two days max. After that, it all goes back to normal again, or at least normal by their standards. Noisy. Chaotic. Every morning.

As it happens, I don't actually have a problem with any of their noisy habits. Just not in the morning, because that is the only time I can sleep. My body finally stops resisting in the morning. When the sun is shining, my eyes will quickly get tired and sleepy, my body ready to rest.

On the other hand, I can hardly ever get to sleep at night, and I can't even have a single dream. My body is always sore and aching from rheumatism. I do have Narsih – my personal nurse – who will give me a massage on my feet, arms and back, but she always does it with a sour face. I don't like that. If she doesn't want or even like doing this, I wish she just wouldn't. The air conditioner that was recently installed in my room means that I frequently need to go to the bathroom. And to do this I have to wake up Narsih, who sleeps in the bed next to me. I can't go by myself because I use a wheelchair.

Waking Narsih up isn't easy. Sometimes she is sleeping so deeply that I have to scream her name in her ear. And after using the bathroom, I get thirsty. So I'll drink a glass of water. Then when I've finished the glass of water, I'll need to go to the toilet again. Back and forth. If I turn off the air con, I'll be too hot. Ah well. So this is old age.

I spend almost every day on my own with Narsih. She looks perfectly pleasant. But if I tell her I urgently need to go to the toilet, her face changes dramatically. She'll purse her lips. When she's cleaning my body, she'll blast the water at me on the strongest setting. She makes me so angry. Once I reminded her that she gets paid to look after me. If she doesn't want to do so, she should just leave. She handed in her notice after that. I was thrilled. But my daughter wasn't happy. She said it's hard to find a good nurse who is patient and gentle. Hah, are we really talking about Narsih? The way she treated me showed me exactly what her qualities were. She's far from nice and gentle. But I had to go along with what my daughter and my son-in-law decided. They are the ones who pay for Narsih, after all.

My daughter asked me why I had to complain about my 'careless nurse', when she and her husband had taken care of all my daily needs, including a private nurse, my own room, a weekly visit from the family doctor, visits to the mall, constant gifts from everyone in our family…

Okay, she's got a point. But the nurse is far more rude than she ever is kind and caring. My room is more like a fridge than a room. When the doctor comes by, he just checks my blood pressure and asks me how I am without even listening to my response. The gifts? Gah, wherever they've been, the gifts are always the same: nappies, a scarf, a comb and a mirror. Sure, so I do use disposable nappies. But that's not a gift – it's a necessity. And then a scarf: where am I going to use such things? Having something wrapped around my neck only makes me overheat. A comb? What do I have to comb? I can count the number of hairs on my head now, all of which are falling out. The more I comb, the more I lose my hair. And then the mirror? That just makes me feel bad about how I look: an old person, wrinkled, toothless and ugly! As for taking me to the mall, well that's just insulting!

They usually have a packed schedule at the weekend. But they also insist on taking me to the famous mall sometimes too. When the day comes, they get so busy and noisy, even more than on the other days. They tell Narsih not to meet her boyfriend or see her family on this day. The driver who usually ends his week on Friday will come in specially at the weekend for me. And then they'll make me go to the toilet a hundred times. 'It's easier to pee at home than in the mall. Such a faff, Bu!' says my daughter loudly. In a high-pitched voice. I often cry after that. Maybe it's because of the way she speaks to me like she's giving a disagreeable command rather than a delicate suggestion; her voice blasts into my ears and rattles my tear ducts. Yes, I am old... All my valves and ducts are loose. Including the tear ducts.

If she sees me crying, she will shout even more loudly: 'What's the matter now, Bu? This is for your benefit. Not mine! If you want to pee in the mall, it will be such a hassle. You will have to get out of your wheelchair and then back in again, and we will have to change your nappy. It would be such a pain. Why are you crying? I'm telling you this for your own good. Less of your whining, please!'

The only one who cares is my granddaughter, who comes into my room and holds me tight whenever she sees me cry. She whispers to me in tiniest voice, 'Please don't cry, Nenek, or I'll start crying too.' I stop when she says that. I don't like to see her round eyes get red. If that happens, her mum will be so mad at me. She will blame me again. I'll cry again. My grandchild will sob. It goes on and on.

Many of my friends have suggested that I just leave. But I won't. Why should I have to leave? They should be the ones to leave: my daughter and my son-in-law should go. I bought this house with my late husband, the father of my children. I own this house. If they want to live here, they should pay me rent. But that's not how it works between children and parents, is it? Not long before my husband passed away, I had a stroke. Before I knew it, I began to depend on them completely. I had to ask them for every little thing I needed. They give me everything I need, but with very bad grace.

This morning: those noisy voices are already filtering through to my room. But they sound much quieter. I move my hands up and down, I cover and uncover my ears: but nothing moves. I slowly move my legs so I don't get a cramp; they don't move either. I try to move my head: still nothing. What's wrong with me?

Those voices are getting further and further away, and then completely vanish. Gone. What's wrong with me? Narsih has woken up so late. She's sitting on the edge of my bed. Staring at me. She looks tired. Then she calls me: 'Nek, Nenek... Please wake up. It wasn't like you not to wake me up to go to the toilet last night, especially since you'd drunk so much water. If only you were like this every night, I wouldn't be so grumpy. We could sleep well. Have lovely dreams. Promise me you'll do the same tonight, okay, Nek? Okay? Nek? Nek!' She calls me many times. I want to turn my head, respond to her: please, no need to scream! I'm not deaf!

Nothing comes out. I can't move my head. What's wrong with me?

Suddenly I can see my own body.

Suddenly I am sitting down next to Narsih. This is amazing!

Suddenly I walk around the room, without needing a wheelchair. This is incredible! Why has this never happened to me before?

Suddenly I see Narsih running out, leaving me in the room. Where is she going? I follow behind her.

Narsih is crying, screaming, sobbing next to the dining table, where my daughter and son-in-law are having their breakfast. My daughter is getting angry. 'What are you on about? I can't understand you if you keep crying like that!'

'Nenek, Bu! Nenek...'

'What's happened?'

'I... Ibu... Nenek.' Narsih is getting more hysterical. My daughter, who has a quick temper, is banging the table. She's shoving Narsih hard to one side. I follow behind her. And when she gets to my room, in front of my bed, she screams, howls, so loud.

She falls down. Her knees hit the floor. She calls me over and over again in between sobs. She moves on her knees, closer to my bed. Holds me. Yes, she's holding me. It's so weird. The door opens, her husband comes into the room. He hugs his wife, asks her to stop crying: 'Stop... Stop... Don't cry. Let her go in peace. Maybe it was her time. Maybe it was for the best for her...' My son-in-law is repeating these phrases. His eyes begin to tear up. My granddaughter is suddenly standing next to my body. She's staring at her parents, and then she starts to cry. Poor little angel. I start to figure out what has happened here: maybe I'm dying now. I am over. The end.

My room is filling up with lots of people. My daughter is still crying. She keeps calling me: 'Bu, please don't leave me...' My son-in-law is busily making all the arrangements, maybe for my funeral. They start to get everything prepared. The living room has been cleaned up, they've put away the couch, prepared long cloths, prayer books with gold covers. Lengths of jasmine are strung up, the pandanus is sliced thinly. The snacks are laid out on the tables. The rented plastic chairs are set up in the courtyard and terrace. All for me. People come and hug my daughter. Comfort her. She whispers to me, 'I've arranged the best funeral for you, Ibu. I want you to be happy...'

In the afternoon, some women in uniforms with headscarves arrive. They sit in a line next to my body. They take a little booklet from their pockets: they say prayers. People are whispering: there will be special prayers on the third day after her passing, then more on the seventh day, and we need to order in food and drink for these days.

I whisper in my daughter's ear, 'I'm not asking for a luxurious funeral with a group of professional prayer-readers in uniform, but for conversations, laughter, sharing stories about what we did together, while there was still time, while I still drew breath, my lovely daughter...' But no one can hear me.

I leave her. Tears rain down her face but they won't bring me back.

ACKNOWLEDGEMENTS

'Ayah, Dini and Him' was first published in *Femina*, the leading women's magazine in Indonesia.

'Maybe Bib was Right' was first published in *Hai*, a magazine for teenage boys.

'Her Mother's Daughter' was first published in *Kompas*, a national newspaper.

'Family Portrait' was first published in *Hai* magazine.

'About Us' was first published in *Femina* magazine.

'24 x 60 x 60' was first published in *Good Housekeeping Indonesia* magazine.

'The Little One' was first published in *Femina* magazine.

'The Trip' was first published in *Femina* magazine.

'Baby' was first published in *Kompas* newspaper.

'Son-in-Law' was first published in *China Moon Journal*.

'Taxi' was first published in *Hai* magazine.

'Dawn on Sunday' was first published in *Hai* magazine

'I Am a Man' was first published in *Spice*, a women's magazine.

'An Apology' was first published in the anthology *Gallery of Kisses*.

'Cik Giok' was first published in *Kompas* newspaper.

'Our World' was first published in *Hai* magazine.

'One Fine Morning' was first published in *Nova*, a tabloid newspaper for women.

ABOUT THE AUTHOR

Reda Gaudiamo is a writer from Jakarta, Indonesia. She was born in 1962 and she wrote her first story when she was in the first grade, reading it to her parents after dinner time. She had her work published for the first time during her time as a French Literature student in the University of Indonesia. She went on to have a successful career in advertising, while continuing to have stories published in national newspapers and magazines.

Her first book – *Bisik-bisik / Whispers* (EKI Press), a short story collection consisting of dialogues – was published in 2004. Since then she has published four collections for adults: *Pengantin Baru / Newly-Weds* (Editum, 2010), *Tentang Kita / About Us* (Stiletto, 2015), *Potret Keluarga / Family Portrait* (2021), and *Hai Nak! / Hey Kid!* (2023).

The Emma Press has published translations of two of Reda's children's novels to date: *The Adventures of Na Willa* (2010) and *Na Willa and the House in the Alley* (2023).

ABOUT THE TRANSLATORS

Ikhda Ayuning Maharsi Degoul is an Indonesian poet from Surabaya, currently based in Ottawa, Canada. Her debut pamphlet, *Ikhda by Ikhda*, was published by the Emma Press in 2014. Her poems have been published in *Mildly Erotic Verse* and *The Emma Press Anthology of Motherhood*. She is co-translator of several books from Indonesian into English, including *The Adventures of Na Willa* by Reda Gaudiamo.

Philippa Barker works as an editor at 3dtotal Publishing, an independent publisher specializing in high-quality art books. When freelancing for the Emma Press, she edited *Once Upon a Time in Birmingham: Women who dared to dream*. She writes short fiction and prose-poetry, and has work published on *Litro, Bare Fiction*, and in *Flash Fiction from the Worcestershire Literary Festival* 2022.

ABOUT THE EMMA PRESS

small press, big dreams

ଔଓ

The Emma Press is an independent publishing house based in the Jewellery Quarter, Birmingham, UK. It was founded in 2012 by Emma Dai'an Wright and specialises in poetry, short fiction and children's books.

In 2020-23 the Emma Press received funding from Arts Council England's Elevate programme, developed to enhance the diversity of the arts and cultural sector by strengthening the resilience of diverse-led organisations.

The Emma Press is passionate about publishing literature which is welcoming and accessible. Visit our website and find out more about our books here:

Website: theemmapress.com
Facebook @theemmapress
Twitter @theemmapress
Instagram @theemmapress

The Adventures of Na Willa

Reda Gaudiamo

Translated from Indonesian by
Ikhda Ayuning Maharsi Degoul and Kate Wakeling

Na Willa is a bright, adventurous girl living in Surabaya's suburbs, her home in the middle of an alley surrounded by cypress trees. She spends her days running after trains, going down to the market, and thinking about how people can sing through radios.

Indonesian author Reda Gaudiamo created a collection of stories of curious adventures and musings of a multicultural girl growing up in Indonesia with an East Indonesian mother and a Chinese-Indonesian father. Set in a time when children spent the day outside, listening to Lilis Suryani's songs on the radio, and when race and gender would still go undiscussed, this is Na Willa's story as she grows up unafraid to ask the big questions.

PAPERBACK ISBN 9781910139592
PRICE £8.99

ALSO FROM THE EMMA PRESS

Tiny Moons
Nina Mingya Powles

Tiny Moons is a collection of essays about food and belonging. Nina Mingya Powles journeys between Wellington, Kota Kinabalu and Shanghai, tracing the constants in her life: eating and cooking, and the dishes that have come to define her.

Through childhood snacks, family feasts, Shanghai street food and student dinners, she attempts to find a way back towards her Chinese-Malaysian heritage.

'Meditative reflections on family, solitude, and belonging, intertwined with mouthwatering descriptions of noodles, dumplings, and sesame pancakes.' *Book Riot*

'Funny, compact and beautifully written.' *New Statesman*

PAPERBACK ISBN 978-1-912915-34-7
PRICE £8.99

How Kyoto Breaks Your Heart

Florentyna Leow

20-something and uncertain about her future, Florentyna Leow is exhilarated when an old acquaintance offers her an opportunity for work and cohabitation in a little house in the hills of Kyoto.

Florentyna begins a new job as a tour guide, taking tourists on elaborate and expensive trips around Kyoto's cultural hotspots. Meanwhile, her relationship with her new companion develops an intensity as they live and work together. Their relationship burns bright, but seasons change, the persimmon tree out back loses its fruit, and things grow strange between the two women.

PAPERBACK ISBN 9781915628008
PRICE £8.99